HAVEN

a novella by
RACHAEL IKINS

Raw Earth Ink

2025

For Jennifer.

First paperback edition July 2025

Cover art by tara caribou

ISBN 978-1-960991-50-8 (paperback)

Published by Raw Earth Ink
PO Box 2
Humboldt, IA 50548
www.raw-earth-ink.com

"There are just bad places. Avoid them."

Trespassers

New Hampshire.

Corey and Sarah giggled as they shared a joint in the cab of Corey's rust bucket Chevy truck. School was out for the summer, and they had been cruising likely spots to park, tunes wailing from the staticky radio. Reception wasn't too good in the mountains. Truck didn't have the glove box port for a USB. They didn't care. Sarah's iPhone was buried deep in her purse.

Too many folks at the lake, among them, Don the mailman's nephew, Jake. He had a huge crush on Sarah. A middle-schooler, he had an unfortunate habit of popping from behind lockers to read her one of the poems he wrote. Sarah punched Corey in the arm any time he made fun of the kid, saying, "You're just jealous."

Nah. He could plunk out a tune on his dad's old Fender, cool enough. All the "arts" he needed.

Down a winding country road, they saw a dilapidated farmhouse with a crooked *For Sale* sign knocked askew by a plow during last year's tough New Hampshire winter. Paint peeled on the house

3

and barn, and the sign hung rusted. Lilacs, chokecherries, and Russian olive competed for space. He pulled the truck around back, careful to stay out of the worst puddles and parked in front of the barn, lights off so no nosy state trooper would see and knock his regulation-issue flashlight against the window. The cab smelled of pot, beer, and sweaty teenage bodies.

Sounds of frogs singing in some unseen pond filled the sweet night air. The truck's engine ticked softly to itself as it cooled. An occasional bat swooped past the windshield searching for early mosquitoes.

"Corey!" giggled Sarah as his hand slid down her arm. She pushed him away halfheartedly, then leaned over to kiss him. He snagged a small square foil packet from his jeans.

She managed to hook one bare foot through the steering wheel, oblivious to the armrest digging into her back. Corey lowered carefully.

Frog song fell silent. A rustling noise drifted in the open windows of the truck as Sarah gasped, "Oh!" Though the armrest digging painfully into her back did not bother, the stealthy sound was like a dash of icy water.

"Stop!" Sarah shouted and pushed his shoulders off. Half-stuck in the steering wheel, she panicked until her foot slid free. "Hear that?"

Corey struggled to reorient himself. "What are you talking about?" he asked and tried to kiss her again.

"NO, stop it! I mean it!" Her eyes were wild as she sniffed the breeze.

He could see their whites in the waning evening

light. He inhaled. "What do you hear?"

Reluctant to open the truck and get out to pull them on standing, he contorted himself into his jeans. Zipping up in the truck door's shelter, Corey heard it. His eyes rolled to the yawn of blackness, the barn entrance. Paralyzed for a moment, his hands fell away from his pants. The rustling grew louder. Sounded like claws.

"Corey!" Sarah laid across the truck bench to reach his shirt. She yanked it over her head. He grabbed the door handle and jumped back into the truck. He was sure he saw something moving in the shadows.

He made a feeble attempt to explain it away. "Dude, it's probably an animal."

"No animals that big around here! Sounds big. Corey!" Tears ran down her face.

"Roll up the windows!!"

They each grabbed an old-fashioned manual handle and punched the locks.

"Let's get out of here."

Sarah shrugged her hoodie around her shoulders. Corey had left the key in the ignition. He was half-afraid this would be like some horror movie and that when he turned it, nothing would happen. But no, the old truck coughed to life. Without fastening seatbelts, he edged down the driveway, bouncing through muddy potholes. Branches snagged the sides of the cab.

Sarah shouted, "What's that?!"

The truck stalled, engine squalling, wheels stuck. They spun deep ruts in mud. Corey switched gears, forward, then reverse. It felt like something had

latched onto a bumper and was trying to drag the truck backwards toward the barn door.

"Step on it!" She grabbed at his arm as he yanked on the gear shift.

Corey stomped his black boot onto the gas pedal. With an angry screech, the truck almost lurched free. Then he looked in the mirror. *Octopus* came to mind. A thick tentacle snaked over the truck bed and tapped delicately at the glass of the back window.

A loud humming noise hurt their ears. Whatever was in the barn was now here. And it was hungry.

Uprooting

Manhattan.

The woman sighed and arched her back, stiff and sore from so much bending over and packing. Again. After her husband had died and she'd made the difficult decision to sell their house and look for a job in the city, she thought she'd stay for good. The animals did not do well with upheaval—she glanced at her fuzzed-out cat clinging to the windowsill off the fire escape and the greying muzzle of her old Lab, Maggie, who snored from a bed the dog had pawed together of clothes Sheryl had worn the day before and her nightgown.

"I don't like upheaval either," Sheryl said aloud to the sleeping dog and stacks of boxes that lurched precariously in piles atop furniture awaiting the movers. But as John Lennon had so aptly put it: "Life is what happens when you are making other plans."

After fifteen years in Manhattan, working for an ad agency, faithfully cranking out lyrics for jingles and wording for ads, Sheryl had gotten a text from her boss, *Come to my office.*

He looked mournful and worn, his long jowls

reminding her of Maggie. Then he said due to budget cuts et cetera, et cetera she was being let go. He'd tried his best with the higher-ups. Blah blah blah.

She sat back on her heels. In two days, the movers would be here bright and early. Once the shock of the ending of her job had worn off, she looked online and found an old farmhouse with a barn and a yard for Mags in New Hampshire. Kind of like the home she and her husband had shared.

Jingles and doggerel for children's cereal boxes sap a writer's creativity. She had other ideas for her writing life. Sheryl was also a poet. Long had she nursed a dream of writing a novel. A place in the country seemed exactly right for it. At fifty-two, she felt like there was no time like the present.

She noticed one box about to tip over that would surely start a landslide. Flat and white with her last name scrawled on it in her husband's writing. It was her wedding dress. She pulled it out of the stack and wiped her sleeve across the clear window so she could look at the garment inside. They had gotten married in the dead of winter, the evening after a day-long blizzard. She hugged the box to her chest and walked over to the window. Trees drooped in late-summer warmth, red maple leaves gone dusty and leathery.

She'd worn her mother's wedding dress, the one in the box she held. Her parents met at Syracuse University back in the '40s. Her mother was an art major, and her father was in the Air Force, stationed at the local airbase. The airmen practiced marching maneuvers on campus. Legend had it that her mother and sorority sisters had been admiring the soldiers from not too far away when her dad's footwear

caught her mom's flirty eye and she'd asked him, "Are those real cowboy boots?" A year later they married. There was little money for wedding frills as the war wound down, so her mother designed her own wedding dress to be sewn from her future pilot-husband's silk parachute.

Her dad had died young almost twenty-five years ago and her mom not long ago at ninety. For a minute, as she contemplated the big change she was about to make and the gamble that she had enough talent left in her to go somewhere with her writing, Sheryl missed them with an acuteness that was physical. She hugged the dress box tightly and whispered, "I love you" to all her lost loves, then set it against the couch.

Missing

New Hampshire.

A few days later, a state police cruiser out on patrol pulled into the driveway of the old house. Both kids' parents had reported them missing. While the authorities considered their ages and tried to assuage parental anxieties with assurances of teenaged hi-jinks, the chief told the officers to keep an eye out.

This morning, the sun shone brightly. With the creak of leather belt, the troopers eased out of their vehicle. An abandoned truck sagged from where it parked halfway out the barn doorway.

"Looks like the boy's truck. Call it in."

While the one spoke into her mic and tapped her dashboard laptop screen, the other walked slowly toward the vehicle. The truck had seen some damage. Cracked windows, bumper hanging off. The rearview mirror lay splintered in a mud puddle, sun cats sparkling off broken edges. He peered into the open cab. Blood.

"We got blood here," he called over his shoulder to his partner. "Let's wait for backup." Back at the cruiser, he eased into the passenger side but left the

door open so he could stretch his legs. He peeled the wrapper off a Slim-Jim and took a bite. Offered it to the other officer as she typed.

"Eeeew, no. Those things are disgusting. Heart-attack on a stick," she said. Laughing, she pushed his hand away. She checked her reflection in the rearview mirror. Sirens whined in the distance. A cold gust blew stuffing from gutted truck seats around the cops' feet. On the other side of the vehicle, a purse, contents strewn in the scraggly grass, gaped open.

Spooked by the sudden movement, he shouted, "This is the police! Corey? Sarah? You kids playing in there? Whoever it is: come out, hands where we can see 'em." He unholstered his pistol and took a step toward the barn.

"I'm waiting right here until the crime scene guys pull in this driveway," his partner said from her side of the cruiser.

Deep ruts lined the driveway. A mystery. Nobody had lived here in forever so who or what dug those grooves? Looked like the kind truck tires would make. Almost as if a tow truck had hauled them out of a ditch only this was a driveway and there was no tow truck.

The smell intensified. Backup spun into the drive, more officers climbing out, holsters unsnapped as they saw the other two, guns drawn.

Body-cams recording, the four advanced into the sunny barn doorway. The smell was bad enough that one ran back outside gagging. The rest covered their faces as best as they could and entered. Just beyond the reach of the sun, they saw an old table, like a wood bench. Blood spattered its surface, some looked black.

"Hey! Get the crime scene techs over here!" Someone's boot hit something mushy. Snapping blue latex gloves on, the officer squatted to reach for it. A woman's summer shoe, green, blood all over, pink-nailed toes still in the straps. He stood up.

"Sarah! Corey!"

A wadded, blood-soaked t-shirt was jammed on the lower shelf of the table. Afternoon peepers and returning redwing blackbirds' song sounded cheerful, an out-of-place soundtrack to what the officers witnessed. A cardboard box teetering on a shelf over the table fell onto it with a soft *bang!* The cops jumped.

"What the hell?" Seed packets of indeterminate age tumbled out. Mouse turds. Someone sneezed.

"Yuck. Put that shit back."

"Musta been knocked when the struggle was going on, maybe." The man's hand stung as he gathered the garbage and shoved the box back on its shelf.

The amount of blood rotting in the sweet spring air left no doubt that the kids were dead. Tracks of raccoons and fox printed the dusty floorboards maroon over black. A dead possum lay decomposing against the wall, everything missing but its naked, broken tail.

Jake Falls in Love

While the young lovers were wrestling with each other and their fears in a driveway of an abandoned farmhouse, thirteen-year-old Jake Willard was upstairs in his room per usual. Alone with his computer, he shut down the game window he'd been in and opened Word. He had an old Dell, a hand-me-down from some cousin or other. It was slow as molasses and kind of ugly, but it was his. He'd plastered the lid with stickers from his favorite graphic novel characters.

He navigated to the most secret file he had. It contained poems. Last year when he started middle school he was put in Advanced English with a new teacher. Nobody liked her much. She was very no-nonsense and treated students as if she expected college-level work. Like everyone else, he was relieved when they moved out of diagramming sentences and other useless grammatical garbage and on to a unit about poetry, even though many people said, "Poetry?" like it was a contagious disease.

Jake's dad, Larry, owned the local juke joint. His mom worked as a front office receptionist in a busy

cardiologists' office one town over from where they lived. Both were "plain, red-white-and-blue Americans" as his dad was fond of saying, doing "simple brown paper work for green pay."

Jake was hard-pressed to find magazines to search for the poems his teacher assigned. She wanted the class to create a three-ring binder notebook on the theme of your choice, and in it you had to glue pages with poems you'd found in magazines and the newspaper and if that failed, she said that it was okay to copy out poems found in books as long as you made sure to credit the author. His mom snagged a pile of ancient Good Housekeepings and Redbooks from her boss's office for him. There were a few poems in them.

The summer he had turned twelve brought strange new feelings. Like at the end of a late afternoon swimming and waterskiing with his cousins and his bestie, when he stripped his suit off with blue wrinkly fingers to dry and get dressed for supper, sometimes a longing would pierce him deep inside, so unearthly and beautiful yet haunting his eyes would fill with tears. He never told his mom about it, but the day Mrs. Gomez sent the class off in search of poems he discovered something. That *yearning* had a language: poetry. Not the rhyming country western stuff his dad listened to coming from coal country down south, but a real language used by real people like Emily Dickinson and Walt Whitman.

Once the notebook project was done, it was followed by memorizing poems from *Reflections on a Gift of Watermelon Pickle* (his favorite was the one where the poet was shaving and thought of a poem

but didn't scribble it on the mirror in soap or pause to jot it down before finishing shaving and lost the poem down the drain forever). Mrs. Gomez's class put on a small performance in the middle school library. Finally, she asked her students to create their own original poems.

Having fallen in love with Emily Dickinson in particular, Jake decided to try to write sort of in her style. He liked free verse.

Mrs. Gomez's eldest son, Jorge, was Jake's BFF. They liked to jump on their bikes in summer to ride out to the old quarry. Some big kid had tied a thick rope to a maple tree that clung to the granite cliffs and the boys delighted in swinging out over the water, hollering like superheroes as they splashed into the depths. Both knew their parents would be horrified if they ever discovered where the boys really went swimming. Innocent faces assured their folks that they met up at the county pool.

One day Jorge (pronounced "Hor-hay" — Jake liked to tease him and call him "Georgie", to which Jorge returned the favor by nicknaming Jake "Hay-kee" even though Jorge spoke with no accent) told Jake his mom was really worried about his grandfather. Later that same week, the phone intercom rang in their classroom during English, and Mrs. Gomez just said, "Yes. Be right there."

She told the class to 'read for fifteen' and left the classroom for the office. Her rapid footsteps echoed in a way Jake found lonely as the sound diminished down the hall. The boys had looked across the room at each other and shrugged. This was the last class of the day so they would catch up later via text message

15

or the online games they played together.

That night, well past bedtime, Jake's phone chirped. He wasn't asleep yet. He propped up on one elbow and tapped the screen.

Jorge. *Meet outside.* Jake's bedroom window opened onto the porch roof. Many times, he had eased the window up so his folks, whose bedroom shared a wall with his, wouldn't hear, and on hot summer nights he'd lie out on the cooling roof to watch for meteors and comets until it chilled him enough for sleep. He shrugged into a shirt hanging off a chair and opened the window. He could see his friend in the dark, a darker shadow in the driveway. He eased onto the roof and then used the drainpipe as a fireman's pole to slide to the ground. They bumped fists and high-fived up-high, down-low as was their habit.

"What's up dude?"

The boys walked to the backyard, out of range of the house.

"Know that phone call my mom got in class today?" Jorge hunched his shoulders into his jacket even though it wasn't very cold out. He shivered. "Well, you know that shit, I mean crap, I mean…"

"Dude, it's *me*, say 'shit', Georgie!"

"Shit!" But Jorge didn't laugh. "That shit on the news about immigration and dreamers and stuff."

"Yeah." Jake's family had immigrated here in the 1700s and 1920s.

"My grandpa might be deported back to Mexico!" His eyes glistened with angry tears which he scrubbed at with one fist.

"Why?" Jake asked loudly then looked over at the silent house praying no lights came on.

"Because my grandpa had his own auto repair and body shop in Mexico. But his dream was to come here and raise his family in the US where there were chances for them to go to college and get better jobs. He came here alone and had to start as a janitor in somebody else's shop. But he saved his money and worked hard and, well, you know his place he has now."

"Everybody knows Lou's!"

"Yeah, well then, he was able to bring my grandma here. My mom was the first person in our family to be born in the United States. I don't really get it but all this SHIT on the news, that asshole president, my grandpa could be deported."

"What does that mean?"

"Sent back to Mexico, forced to leave Grandma who is sick. *Buelo* isn't so strong anymore himself."

"Why?"

"Because my mom and my Tio Gonzalo are the only citizens in my family. My grandparents worked so hard *Abuelito* never got around to applying for his citizenship."

"But I thought in civics class, Mr. Albright said that the parents of kids who are born here, having a kid allows them to stay."

"Dunno now. I feel sick to my stomach. My mom cried all through dinner." Even though they were older dudes at thirteen, not little kids anymore, Jake hugged his friend. He could feel Jorge's shoulders shaking with the effort not to cry.

"I gotta go home. But thanks, 'mano. I just had to talk about it."

Jake stood in the driveway for a long while

watching his friend's shadow dwindle under the streetlight and finally become one with the night. He climbed back up to his room and lay awake on his bed for most of the night, hands clasped behind his head, wishing he could help. He thought back to the English class unit on poetry and what had happened when it was time to write their own.

Some kids were jerks and asked dumb questions about what to write. Now Jake understood better why Mrs. Gomez hadn't been impatient but had said, "A dream you have that sustains you. That is the topic."

Some dork in the back had piped up, "Like a dream when you're sleeping?"

Mrs. Gomez was undeterred. "Yes," (only she pronounced it "jess") "Those kinds of dreams are also good subject matter. I meant, for example, if you wanted to go to college, but you knew you didn't have enough money, so you worked after school and summers to save up to realize your dream."

Jake's hair made a swishing sound as he shook his head into his pillow. No bigger dream than coming to a foreign country and trying to make it.

As Mrs. Gomez had made her way up the rows while students sweated over their compositions, he'd hunched his shoulders protectively when he felt her hand on the back of his chair. Sweat popped out along his hairline and he felt one drop trickle down his rib cage. She read. He held his breath. He prayed he didn't have BO.

"Jake, you know what," she spoke with that slight accent.

He shook his head.

"You are a poet. There is no doubt in my mind. This is wonderful, especially the way you connect your imagery to the emotion in this piece. Nice job."

Now he was sweating everywhere as his heart pounded with joy. He looked down at his smudged paper and the few words on it. *She says I am a poet. I am good at this.* He floated home that day. Couldn't wait to tell his mom.

As soon as she had put away her coat and bag and grabbed a seltzer from the fridge, Jake sat with her at the table. When she asked how was school, he carefully pulled the sheet with the smudged lines Mrs. Gomez liked so much and started to push it across the table. Then he changed his mind and pulled it protectively to him.

"What's that?" she chuckled.

"I wrote a poem in English class today. My teacher thinks it's really good." He looked at his mother from under his downturned brows.

She swallowed some seltzer and then clasped her hands. "Okay, will you read it to me? I'm all ears." One thing about his mom confused him, he never was quite sure if she was making fun of him or if comments like that were just her idea of a joke.

"Umm, okay. I guess." He held the paper trembling in front of him, cleared his throat and when he began, his voice cracked. Red to the tips of his ears and top of his sweating head, he didn't look at his mother; he knew she would be grinning — and started again.

"Oh, honey," she said sounding genuinely impressed. "That is beautiful. Why don't we hang it

on the fridge?"

"Aw, Mom, no! I'm not a little kid and this is way more important than some kid drawing of a house or something. I want to be a poet! I am one. Gonna go to college for it and be a writer."

His mother sighed and sipped her drink. With great care, for she recognized vulnerability and wasn't as insensitive as her son suspected, she said, "Well, that certainly is a dream. You're going to be the first guy in our family to be a university man. But you can't be a poet. No money in it. You know as well as I do that your dad won't pay for college unless you do what he wants."

There would be student loans and financial aid as well but, yes, Jake knew what his dad wanted; a major in accounting and then come home and run that end of the bar business.

"Mom," his chair legs screeched as he bolted upright jostling the seltzer on the table. "I suck at math!!! I hate it!! I am *not* going to college to be a boring old accountant. I love poetry! I love writing. My teacher says I have a real talent." Those last words thrown over his shoulder as he raced upstairs before she could see his tears.

His mom shook her head sadly to the empty kitchen. They had a few years before Jake needed to start applying to colleges. Who knew, maybe her husband would come around. *Yeah, right,* she thought. *And the moon will turn out to be made of Swiss cheese inhabited by astronaut mice in teeny weeny space suits.*

Behind his closed door, under the watchful eyes of his old Spider-Man poster, Jake started to wad the

paper into a ball to throw out, debated tearing it into a million strips, but then gently smoothed it over his knee and soundlessly read the words again. His fingers gently stroked the small patch of stubble that had recently begun to sprout on his upper lip and a few hairs on his chin. Not enough to shave but it counted.

When his dad got home at six o'clock, grabbing a quick bite and burying himself behind the sports section of the paper before racing back to work, Jake's mom said, "Honey, Jake wrote a poem in English class today. A real poem. His teacher likes it a lot."

His dad bent down the top of the newspaper and looked over at his son. "Did ya now?" He disappeared again.

Jake's heart sank and he threw his mom a desperate, "why did you have to say that" look.

Unperturbed, his mom said, "Jake why don't you go get it and read it to us. I'd love to hear it again."

Inwardly the boy groaned, and hung his head. He didn't have to go anywhere. He eased the carefully folded paper from the back pocket of his jeans.

"C'mon, please listen to him," his mom begged his dad, who, with a put-upon sigh, folded the newspaper.

"Alright, get with the program. I have to get back to work."

When Jake finished the last word, not a sound could be heard in the kitchen except the *tick-tock* of the old clock which hung over the fridge.

"Hmph," his dad said. "I don't like it. It's not poetry. Doesn't rhyme. Poetry rhymes and that's

that." He opened the paper again.

"You don't know anything, Dad," said Jake quietly, his heart breaking. "It's free verse. You don't even know what that is. All you listen to is country western music. Some of those lyrics might be poetry, but there is way more to it than that. I am going to be a writer."

His father slammed the newspaper onto his lap and leaned forward. "The hell you are! You're going to get a decent American job in accounting and make a decent paycheck and none of this poetry shit. I won't discuss it anymore. Poetry is for fags and wussies."

He thumped out the back door, jingling his truck keys as Jake double-stepped up the stairs and banged his door shut so hard the fan fell out of his bedroom window.

He didn't see his mother's stricken expression. She had hoped that her husband might've seen past his own limitations, well, past his bigotry and ignorance, to be honest. She felt bad she had asked their son to read his precious poem. To leave himself open. She sighed and finished loading the dishwasher.

A Father's Disapproval

New Hampshire, A Year Later.

She was staring out the window over the sink, her hands in soapy water when the phone rang. Normally Jake would hit the floor and race to see the caller ID and answer if it was one of his buddies. Not this time, silence overhead. The ongoing fight over Jake's future, or as she called it in her head "The Poetry Wars", had just concluded the latest battle. She saw it was her brother, Don Cobb. He worked as a letter carrier at their local post office.

"Hey there."

"Howdy sis, how's it goin'?"

"Oh, could be better, could be worse," she sighed.

"What's wrong? C'mon spill," Don said to his little sister.

"Oh, just Jake and Larry fighting again. Teenage stuff." She tried to laugh. "What can I do for you?"

"It is Jake I called about. I think I found him a part time after-school job. Wanted to know if he's interested."

"Why don't you try his cell or text him? He's

barricaded in his room right now. His dad really hurt his feelings."

Their conversation dwindled and Don said he would do just that.

What About the Haven House

The house that went with the barn where Corey and Sarah had disappeared was the old Haven place, though nobody alive could remember when a Haven had last lived there. It moldered in the sun and rain, peeled its paint, and the realty sign listed even further toward the ditch as gravity called to it. The yellow crime scene tape faded and tore and the murder of Corey and Sarah remained unsolved.

At the post office, Don Cobb, uncle of Jake the Poet, was scanning and filing letters as they came along the belt. He pondered the Haven house because he'd just received a forwarding order. Some woman from downstate New York had bought it. He turned to his coworker Candice.

"You ever know anybody who lived out at the Haven place?"

"Seriously, Don?" she asked as she stamped a package on her scale. "With three kids and a wife who drives truck and is away more than home, you think I have time to ponder the history of that old dump?" She laughed as she reached for the next package.

"When you think about it, can't recall a name or

25

face of anybody who ever lived there. Dunno there ever *was* a Haven." He shook his head considering this. Seemed like there was a strangeness associated with the property. He knew he had to have delivered mail there sometime in his thirty years as a postal worker, but for the life of him he couldn't think of any families – not names or faces.

In October, commuters driving by the old farmhouse where the unsolved murder happened began to notice changes. Everyone wondered who would buy a murder-house. Someone from out of town most likely. First off, the real estate sign was set straight, a "sold" sticker on it. Before you knew it, someone had mowed the lawn and a few days later, on a Wednesday afternoon, a U-Haul was parked in the driveway and several beefy-looking guys were unloading boxes and furniture.

A woman climbed out of a red Jeep Cherokee parked in front of the barn right over the now-filled-in ruts Corey's truck had gouged in the dirt. She walked an elderly Labrador-mix on a leash. A cat curled up in a carrier on the front seat, peering out the window atop a stack of boxes.

The guys down at Tom's Farm and Garden who daily drove past there studied all of this with interest and reported on the daily changes at Larry's Bar and Juke Joint, which was owned by Jake's dad, an establishment so disgusting your boots made sticky sounds as you walked across the floor but after enough beer, nobody cared.

Transplanted to New Hampshire

The stranger was a writer from New York City. Rumor spread via grass roots telegraph that she had lost her job due to alcohol... drugs... a bad love affair? And had come here to write the great American novel. Her dog, named Maggie, black with whitened muzzle, had a tendency to wag her tail so hard against door frames, sometimes it bled. Always with that goofy Labrador smile while making tiny chuffing noises of joy, deep in her throat. Also, said experts at Larry's, she had a cat. Maybe a fat calico or a rescue tabby to sit in the paint-peeling windows of the old house, saying "ack ack ack" to birds on the new feeder the woman had hung from a spruce tree.

"What'd you do?" demanded Larry of a patron one night as he pulled a beer. He eased up on the tap as the foam slid down the side of the glass. "Standin' up by her window were ya, checkin' her out with your binoculars?" This bit of wit was greeted with laughter among the regulars seated there.

Eventually the U-Haul had driven away, and the

woman started to show up at the farmer's market and Tom's store in town, laying in supplies for her new digs. Seemed kind of standoffish. City-folk, what can you do? In a small town, everybody knows everybody, and it's more like a family.

She had lost her job through no fault of her own, laid off, budget cuts, slow economy. At age fifty-two, finding something new in the advertising world, in any world, was much harder. Besides, writing jingles was not what she'd majored in creative writing to do. Her real love was poetry. Most companies wanted a fresh young face to put their stamp on and who could be paid far less than a longtime experienced worker. She had always wanted to write, did write, scribbled bits of poetry and short fiction. She had hung out at open mics and library writing groups in the city.

Another dream was to write a novel. It seemed to her, a decent novel was a more respectable way to pay the bills and support the poetry than advertising. Reality was rejections piling up over the years. She decided the day her boss called her into his office to give her the bad news, to chuck the city altogether and find some old farmhouse in New England, somewhere to renovate, recharge her batteries, and write that novel. Besides, she wanted to give her faithful old Maggie a yard of her own to run around in while Maggie still was able to chase rabbits.

Her name was Sheryl. She trimmed the weeds from around the mailbox, thinking of planting a clematis there next spring, bought some black paint, and one Indian summer morning after breakfast, carefully painted the box and then glued the white stick-on letters of her last name on it. Perkins. She

stepped back onto the sandy shoulder of the road to admire her work. She laughed. Lettering was not her strong suit. Crooked but legible.

The mailman had already left her a pile of mostly junk and some envelopes affixed with the yellow forwarding address labels. She bent down and looped her hand through the paint can, mindful of the sound of a vehicle coming around the curve. The signature New Hampshire granite boulders that rose like the bones of the earth, furred with deciduous trees and evergreens - dark green hair on a stone skull - created an echo chamber. The oncoming traveler's rumbling vehicle sounded familiar. She glanced at her watch. Yep, mailman. Thinking of the devil. She grinned and waved as he drove past on his way to a special delivery.

He had caught a glimpse of her in his rearview mirror on move-in day. Now, Don Cobb didn't listen to half the gossip of the town chin-waggers so he was open-minded as to what the stranger was like. He figured anyone on her own and in a new place might be a tad shy. He noticed she stood about five foot five and probably weighed around one fifty. Comfortable, with soft edges. Her hair bushed out in a silvery curly mass, and she wore glasses and a lot of silver jewelry, dangly earrings, bracelets and whatnots. No makeup. Women didn't need makeup in his opinion. It was just a ploy by big corporations to sell cosmetics and get rich. He liked the gentle way she stroked her dog, and he liked some of the changes she was making to the sad old farmhouse.

One day he pulled into the driveway on impulse. He cooked up some story about a package as he

climbed the creaking front steps and put his finger to the doorbell.

Sheryl happened to be unpacking boxes in the kitchen. At the sound of the bell, Maggie heaved herself to her paws and trundled to the foyer. "It's okay, Mags." Sheryl unlatched the door and pulled it open to find the mailman standing there. His name, Don, was stitched onto the chest pocket of his uniform. He smiled and stuck out his hand. Hers were all dirty from unpacking boxes, but she wiped them on her jeans and shook it. He had warm brown eyes.

"Wanted to welcome you to the neighborhood," Don said, squatting down to scratch Maggie behind the ears. She smiled and wagged.

"Thanks," said Sheryl. "I can only offer you a cup of coffee," she laughed. "I have gotten as far as unpacking the Chemex and mugs."

"Naw, that's okay," replied Don. "I have to get back to my route. Oh, here," he reached into his mail pouch and handed her a stack of letters bound with a rubber band. "And I didn't forget you," he assured Maggie who was wagging with canine optimism. From a side pocket he produced a biscuit which she took very gently with her lips and then, toenails clicking on the hardwood floor, she stumped back to the kitchen to savor it on her dog bed.

Don noticed a tabby cat peering out from behind the banister on the stairs. He reached back in another side pocket and produced an envelope of Friskies Treats. "Here you go," he extracted one shaped like a fish and extended it slow and easy-does-it toward the cat. She glared at him with dilated pupils but sniffed. He set the treat in front of her and pulled his hand

away. As soon as nobody was watching, Girlie crunched the treat.

"You've done it now," Sheryl laughed. "Maggie'll be trying to get into your truck next time, and she will beg to be let out when she knows it is time for you to come by."

"That's okay by me," Don grinned at her. "She's a nice old gal. Sweet that you have a yard for her to run around in. I bet once she sees her first squirrel, she'll turn quite spry. Don't be letting that nice kitty out though. Coyotes and foxes around here. They might grab her." The cat permitted a stroke on her head.

"Oh, no. Girlie is strictly an indoor cat. We lived in an apartment three floors up in a big building. She's never been outside further than a windowsill with a screen in it."

She opened her mouth, then hesitated. Don stood patiently, wondering what she wanted to say. She spoke, the words coming out in a rush.

"The day my boss called me into his office was a really bad day. I hadn't been generating many new accounts—I worked for an ad agency in NYC and wrote jingles, you know like the silly one on TV for laundry detergent that gets into your head and becomes an ear worm?"

Don laughed. He'd never heard the term 'ear worm' before but he knew just what she meant.

"There had been budget cutbacks and staff layoffs. It's hard to compete in such a technological world where everybody and his brother is self-producing on YouTube and the internet. Besides, writing drivel like that was not my dream job." She

chuckled self-consciously and pushed her hair behind her ears. The bracelets jingled.

Don sat down, and she did too, pulling up a chair at the kitchen table which was covered with junk from unpacking.

"I saw his face," she continued, "And my heart sank. Dream job or not, it paid the bills. But after he lowered the boom, cowardly ass couldn't even look me in the eye and I'd worked there fourteen years. I gathered my coat and purse to head home. As I walked to the parking garage where my car was, I suddenly felt as if a weight had fallen off me, one I hadn't known was even there. I really don't like the city. Never have. My dog," here she paused to bend over and hug Maggie to her knees, "Was growing older and she has never had a yard of her own. Since a puppy, it was leashes all the time. So, I thought maybe we could find a house in the country."

"And here you are!" said Don.

Sheryl laughed. "Yes, for better or worse, we are indeed here."

"I'm so glad! This sad old house could use some love. You know the history, right?"

Sheryl cocked her head, eyebrow raised.

Don continued "Oh, well, not sure if I should say, but, well, I've already started something, haven't I? So, a couple summers ago a couple of teenage kids were found murdered outside the barn."

Sheryl's mouth made a perfect o.

"Wow, so you didn't know. Well, their bodies weren't ever found, really. And the case was never solved. Place has stood empty... until now. Looks like both you and the house have been through tough

times. Welcome. Best be on my way." Don clanked his keys feeling embarrassed and uncomfortable and stepped off the porch.

As he climbed into the mail truck, he turned and waved. Sheryl was still standing in the open door of the house, a greenish shadow across her face. He shivered for no good reason. Maples rustled in the breeze, preparing to let go of their burden of orange, red, and gold leaves. He called, "See you all tomorrow."

Sheryl shut the door on the sound of his vehicle trundling down the country road. She and Maggie looked at each other. "A murder. Hmm. Double. I wonder why the realtor never said. Maybe I can look it up online."

Maggie wagged encouragement.

"On the other hand," her fingers rubbed behind the dog's ears in just the right spot, "It doesn't really matter, does it? Something about this place, when I opened the car door and let the air in, it spoke to me, pulled me right out. And when the real estate agent unlocked the front door, there was a scent of cedar, and the way the sunlight slanted across the floor. As if the house had hugged me in big arms and said 'you are home.'" Maggie rolled onto her back. "I don't ever want to leave. I think I want to be buried here."

Sheryl needed someone or something to nurture. She'd lost her husband and mother and the job she'd held for most of her adult working life in a city where anonymity rushed people past without seeing them. She needed roots. In the Haven house, it appeared she would be able to sink them deep.

While his emotions settled as he drove back to the post office, Don had an inspiration. Maybe that could make up for his unfortunate gaffe. To be fair, he knew someone would have eventually spilled the beans about the history of the Haven house. Tonight, he'd give his nephew Jake a call, see if he had any free time. Maybe Jake would ride on over and offer to help the new neighbor around her yard.

Besides, he grinned into the rearview mirror of the truck, *Jake writes poetry. I bet I can get him to show her some. Few he's read me are pretty damned good, never mind what my brother-in-law says.*

Maggie and a Yard of Her Own

One morning, not long after they'd moved in, Sheryl let Maggie out by herself for her morning business while she made coffee and watched from the window over the stove.

Maggie sniffed and slowly meandered, nose to ground, pausing to chew succulent "rabbit raisins," as Sheryl called them. Maggie's path after these treats led her toward the barn and the next time the dog looked up, the open door was right in front of her.

She sniffed and looked over her shoulder guiltily at the house. Something felt off here. Something smelled… *bad*. Not the good kind of bad when a dog would throw herself onto something rotten to rub that gorgeous stench deep into her fur, no, this was bad like Maggie's memory of her dog-friend Aidan. He was always tied to a porch, and last winter nobody brought him inside when the temperatures dipped low enough that Maggie's feet stung to walk, and she limped when she had to do her business.

Aidan froze to death. Dogs know that magic is real, of both the white and black kinds, and Maggie wondered if some evil spell had befallen Aidan's

human that caused her to forget about him. She remembered Sheryl crying as Maggie leaned against her knee while they watched the awful story on the news.

Maggie's job, one of them, besides carrying balled up dirty socks to the laundry basket and licking plates and bowls clean, was protector. She didn't want to, but she forced herself to enter the barn. Her legs, which were stiff with age, grew even stiffer, as if on their own they were trying to keep the dog out of there.

Just inside the door, everything was dark. Maggie couldn't see in the dark like Girlie, so she used her nose. She sneezed violently. Yuck. Yes, over there something about that table with old cardboard boxes on it and the shelves on the wall. She inched closer. Her hackles rose and suddenly she was growling and backing up. The *bad* was there. She heard Sheryl's voice.

"Maggie, chow time! Mags, where are you?"

With a last glance into the shadows, she turned and trotted out, promising herself to come back and see if whatever is it was, was something she could attack and chase away.

Sheryl Remembers a Friend

Job loss wasn't the only reason Sheryl had moved her little family far from the city. She stood in the kitchen surrounded by a sea of cardboard boxes. The sound of that foolscap wrapping paper was driving her nuts as she unwrapped her belongings. She had lost her best friend too.

They'd met over a project, Sheryl doing the writing and Lana the graphic design. Friendship sparked between them and over the months they confided their life stories in each other, often sharing a fresh baguette melting with butter and cups of espresso at a café that became *their place*.

Lana tended to affect, or so it seemed at first, large-framed round sunglasses and beige or white turtlenecks with black jackets no matter the weather, even in summer. Until the afternoon Sheryl went to the ladies' room and surprised Lana with her sunglasses off, leaned forward gingerly pressing a swollen, green and purple black eye. They were good enough friends that Sheryl just looked at her friend and Lana did not immediately put the glasses back on.

Their eyes me in the mirror. "Who did that to you?" Sheryl was not one to mince words.

Lana rooted through her purse and opened the makeup compact she pulled out, smearing a new layer over the purple as best she could. "It's nothing."

"Nothing? Is it your husband? What else does he do to you?" Sheryl gently pulled down the neck of Lana's shirt and revealed more bruising. Her friend hugged herself and it became apparent that she also had injured ribs.

"I went to the emergency room last night. I had to, the bleeding…"

Sheryl locked the bathroom door. "Go on."

"The ER doctor was so nice." Lana's eyes welled with unshed tears. "He told me he would stand by me, they all would. It's a law or something. That they'd call social services."

"Why didn't you do it?"

"Oh, Brett doesn't mean it. He just gets so frustrated with his job and he's always so tired."

"Damn, girl, he does mean it. Nobody rational does this out of frustration. One day he could kill you!"

Lana had made some vague reference to her kids, ten and twelve, a girl and boy and then somebody started to knock on the bathroom door.

Sheryl did her best to be non-judgmental and supportive, reading all she could on spousal abuse. She tried to encourage her friend to take the kids and leave, told her about safe houses and all. Time passed, more turtlenecks and glasses, and then the day when Lana confessed that the night before, during an especially bloody battle, the kids had run to the

kitchen, taken chef's knives from the knife drawer, screaming in defense of their mother. Still, she stayed, paralyzed.

For Sheryl, that was the breaking point of her heart; she had to let the friendship go. She explained with as much love as she could that she couldn't be a part of watching the abuse, her friend injured, and possibly killed. She wasn't sleeping over this.

Lana had smiled sadly and just walked away.

Sheryl wondered, as she rooted in a box, if Lana was still alive. She set a small ceramic jar with a Picasso-style cartoon cat on its rotund belly on the counter. Lana had given her that.

The Old Barn

One day, Sheryl avoided writers' block by simply not writing at all and gave in to her increasing fascination with the barn, much to Maggie's consternation. Sheryl shrugged into her denim jacket and went to investigate the barn. She discovered what must've been a tack room, wood pegs on the wall to hang tack. Other rooms had obviously held cattle. One, walls only shoulder height, bore scars gouged into the wood from what might've been the horns of an ornery bull. Three rickety wooden stanchions stood in a row and next to them a small room with a splintered door — calf pen, she figured.

Among other rustic items, she found a bizarre sign from an old livestock auction house stating on its faded pink paper *Cattle Wanted - Dead or Alive*. Whew. There was a lovely old spatterware enamel colander hanging off a beam. She appropriated this for kitchen use and as a decoration over her sink. What would've been the hay mow held nothing but a rotted rope net hanging up high toward the roof peak. Pigeons flew in and out of the tiny window.

Maybe she could use the floor of it as a garage.

A center chamber still contained a worn leather harness for a double team of horses or mules. Must've been their stall, hay rick rotting on one wall. Outside that door she found a rusty gray tin barrel with a funny half-hooded lid.

She'd looked up similar items on an antique site online and learned it was a chicken feeder circa 1930s. Set upside down, feed would've poured into the hood and the chicks could've pecked in it at will. She dragged the barrel out into the sun. Maybe she'd paint it and plant something in it, a red cascade of geraniums or something. Or maybe, who knew, this city girl might research keeping chickens and have a few for fresh eggs and as garden insect-eaters.

Long time ago, in what felt like another whole other life, when her husband was alive, they had raised chickens. He had been her biggest poetry fan, never too busy to stop what he was doing if she asked him to listen to a new composition. There was that March when she and their pet potbelly pig Rosie had walked to the mailbox and in it was an announcement that she had won first prize in the first ever contest she'd entered. She had tripped and whooped up the driveway, her big rubber boots almost doing her in. Her husband had turned from the sink where he was washing up the dinner dishes, his eyebrows raised. She had thrown herself into his arms waving the letter around his head. When she could speak and showed it to him, they both cried. She shook herself... long time ago.

There was an old shed listing near the barn which, upon closer inspection, looked to have been the chicken coop, but the stairs going to the upper

41

level were rotted through. She decided if she ever did buy herself some chicks, she'd also order a prefab chicken coop on Amazon and house them that way.

As she left the barn, she decided there must be plenty of decent subject matter for stories in that old building's walls for her to write about.

Winter in the Country

Winter came, and with it, heavy snows. Sheryl adjusted to keeping a wood stove stoked and wore layers of heavy sweaters and long underwear. In the city, winter was more an inconvenience than anything. Here, where she was more isolated than most on a winding country road, she had had to think ahead for the days when even the Cherokee wouldn't be able to negotiate drifts and stock up on canned goods and pet food. Thank goodness for *Chewy.com*! They delivered pet supplies in all weathers.

Since they'd moved in in the fall, she hadn't had much time for stockpiling. Come spring, she dreamt of planting a big vegetable garden and buying herself a small freezer and a canner so that she could put up a lot of her own food for the following winter.

She had no family left. Well, her cousins but they lived in Seattle. Her mom had taught her how to can so long ago, and other now seemingly amusing "wifely" skills like how to iron a collar on a man's dress shirt, how to hang shirts and pants on the clothesline correctly, and that you do your vacuuming first and then dust the furniture. Sheryl

chuckled. In truth her mother had not been keen on house cleaning and in her later years had luxuriated by hiring a cleaning lady.

Sheryl's mother had died two years previous, right around Sheryl's birthday. Her mom was ninety. That last spring, she had begun to complain of back pain. With a history of falls, osteoporosis and arthritis, and having spent too many summers laid up in rehab centers, her mom seemed destined for yet another stint in one. Sheryl helped her with heating pads on the sore places and asked her what she wanted to do. Four months later, when her mom's skin had turned almost mustard yellow, Sheryl insisted she take her to a gerontologist, who diagnosed pancreatic cancer.

Sheryl stopped what she was doing with boxes and stared out the window. To this day she had to stop herself from reaching for the phone to call her mother. She wondered if that ever went away.

What an awful time that had been. She had brought Maggie and Girlie and they moved in the last weeks of her mom's life. In spite of everything, the two had had some good conversations that would sustain Sheryl all of her days as her mom grew worse, bleeding under the skin, even her eyes yellow. They called Hospice. Against feeble argument, Sheryl installed her mom as comfortably as she could on a recliner in the living room. There was the DNR hanging off the fridge for the ambulance guys should someone call them, even though nobody was supposed to.

Sheryl held the woman who had seemed like a force of nature in her arms, naked, on a portable potty when the visiting nurses ran to get a fresh night gown.

She remembered cradling her head against her breasts—Sheryl's lack of a bra ever a source of argument in better times—and telling her mom, "I've got you. Rest your head against my boobs, they are soft and warm."

The first time Sheryl had heard an owl hunting after they'd moved into the farmhouse, she thought of the owls in the blue spruce along the driveway of her mother's house. She'd taken Maggie out one last time that sad night and heard them courting in the tree. She'd run into the house calling, "Mom, Mom!" By some miracle her mother's eyes had opened. Owls were believed to be spirit guides when someone dies. Sheryl and her mother and dad had shared a passion for nature and birdwatching. Her mother had opened her eyes and then she was gone.

Carefully she stacked plates and bowls that her mom had gifted her in her new kitchen cabinets.

Late Winter - Rainy Days
Before the First Spring

Rain streamed down the windows. She wished it could wash away the certain memories, pictures in purple and yellow best forgotten. She consciously tried to replace the images with memories of her mother raking up sticks in spring or her mom applying lipstick before going grocery shopping. Or sniffing the winter coat Sheryl had kept and sometimes wore that still, in the right weather, had the faintest fragrance, a conglomeration of perfume, cigarette smoke, and lipstick that was the scent of *Mom*.

The next time she was able to spend an hour or so in the barn wasn't until early spring, April 2nd. Maggie avoided it and hoped that Sheryl forgot it was there. Snow had begun to melt, and musical streams of water poured off roof and ledge. The path she had shoveled for Maggie from the back door to the driveway showed bare earth.

While she rummaged in the barn under the weak sunshine, she found a crumbly cardboard box, grainy

with layered dust, on a shelf above a rickety work bench. The dog whined and in the house the cat fuzzed up her tail and jumped hissing from the window to hide under an upstairs bed.

A Discovery

Sheryl sat down on an old damp-from-melted-snow lawn chair and wiped the dust off the flaps. She took off her mittens. Opened the box. Unable to look away even though thunder grumbled, she reached in. Some nameless unpleasant bugs scrabbled over her hand. She screamed, a short soft blast. The dog whined. She pulled out several seed packets of questionable history, most chewed by mice, contents eaten. There was a scent on the air of decay as she brushed off mouse droppings and mouse fluff. She coughed.

At the very bottom of the box, half stuck under a flap, she discovered one packet of seeds. The lettering on the faded envelope was in some foreign language she couldn't read. She assumed, judging by a painted image the general shape of a squash and the faint sick-green tone of the paint used to illustrate it, that these must be some exotic zucchini seeds. Later, she'd google that lettering, see if she could find out what language it was. Way older than heirloom. Maybe brought over with immigrants long ago. The envelope was so fragile, the paper almost disintegrated in her

48

hands. She could tell right away, due to the rattle and bulge, some seeds were probably still intact.

Other torn packets in the box had been eaten by mice and she startled and said, "Eeeeww" when she found a little dead body and bones. She slipped a dirty fingernail under the flap and sneezed.

She shook the seeds gently into her other palm. There was a shocking tingle where they touched her skin, a grasp or pull, as if they were mosquitoes, trying to suck their way in to her blood. She dismissed this thought as ridiculous, spread the seeds onto a paper plate from yesterday's lunch on the garden table next to her lawn chair and looked around the yard. One hand reached down absently to pet the dog's head, but Maggie had long since bolted for the open kitchen door, whites of her eyes showing, tail between her legs.

"Silly girl," mumbled the writer. She stood up, slapped her hands on her already dirty jeans and ambled back into the barn to grab a shiny new trowel from the battered wooden workbench she had now claimed as a garden station. She neglected to pull on the also new garden gloves next to it on the shelf. She again pondered the strange lettering on the antique packet.

Planting a Garden:
Sheryl Meets Jake

Once the snows of winter had vanished (it had been an unusually rainy and cool spring) so glad was she to be out of the city and have a house and garden of her own, she made quite an inroad on the brambly tangle of weeds and shrubs surrounding her new home. She mapped out an area for a small vegetable garden using the orange stakes that had previously stood in the driveway to show the plow guy where the edges were. She added fencing to her list for the farm and garden supply store, to prevent rabbits and deer from sampling the contents. Spray was also added for whatever insects consumed the leaves of the small Cherokee purple tomato plant and the Old German heirloom with orange flesh and others she had already planted, and then she sprinkled a repellant sure to keep out all warm-blooded marauders who would enjoy vegetable seedlings around the entire garden. She kept a clear plastic tarp to drape over the fence like a tent, if the forecast predicted a late frost.

One evening as the sun set, there was a knock on the front door. Sheryl was in the kitchen washing up the supper dishes, pesto and salad. Maggie woofed to her feet and stomped importantly to the door, wagging her tail, glancing over her shoulder at Sheryl.

"I'm coming, old girl." Sheryl unlocked the dead bolt and opened the door. A teenaged kid stood there, a young man. Red hair, freckles interspersed with a few spots, Adam's apple bobbing in a neck that had already begun to show firm muscles. He didn't have to shave much yet.

"Hi. Help you?" They both spoke at once and both laughed. Sheryl stood back from the door and gestured him to come in as he squatted down to scratch Maggie behind the ears.

"Come all the way in! Don't want the cat to escape." Maggie and the boy moved into the foyer. He stood up. She looked into clear green eyes and an open sensitive face. She recalled meeting him briefly some weeks past in her driveway. His name escaped her.

"My name is Jake," he offered, sticking out his hand for her to shake. "You know Don? The mailman? He's my uncle. Let me just take off my shoes."

"Oh, oh nice to see you again." Sheryl shook his proffered hand. "I remember you… What can I do for you?" She noticed him reach back and pat his back pocket.

"Umm?" he cleared his throat. "Well, Uncle Don said maybe as you could use some help out here cleaning up the yard or the barn. I came to see," his

voice trailed off and, true to many redheads, the poor boy blushed to the roots of his hair.

Sheryl walked to the window and looked out. He'd leaned his bike against the porch railing. "You know, that would be really great. Some of that stuff in the barn is really heavy. You any good with busting sod and shoveling?"

"Sure… I write poetry, too." *Oh shit*, thought Jake. *I can't believe I just blurted that out.* He shuffled his sneakers. His face felt like it was on fire.

"You do? What a coincidence. I write it, too. Or used to." Sheryl shrugged into her old coat. "Let's go out to the barn before it gets much darker. You could come back in the morning. It's Saturday. Supposed to be a decent day. Here, Maggie." She clipped the leash onto the bouncing dog's collar, "Let's go pee-pee."

She held the door open for Maggie who bolted surprisingly fast for an old lady and then Jake, who clumped after her.

Maggie Worries

The following weekend, while Sheryl dug the preliminary patch and Jake set out the boundary of cedar planks for her raised vegetable garden, Maggie lay in the kitchen doorway, head on paws, whitened eyebrows pinched together in a frown of doggy anxiety.

Meanwhile, as spring neared the magical planting date of Memorial Day weekend, writer-woman in her Wellington boots with grass clippings up the sides, her face smeared with sun block – because "we aren't kids any more to go mindlessly naked into the outdoors," and bug-spray to ward off mosquitoes, black flies, and ticks and the ever-increasing numbers of illnesses they carry blared about on the nightly news – continued to work outside.

Maggie would struggle to stay awake, thinking she should get up and snatch the packet of seeds away from her beloved woman and carry them into the woods to bury them far away. But she was so tired. Her eyelids drooped.

The boy continued to come on the weekends,

riding up on his bike, dropping it in the front yard. Maggie wondered why he didn't notice the bad smell that lingered. Maybe only dogs could. It smelled like danger.

The Seed Packet

The night Sheryl tried to research the lettering on the packet, something was wrong with the Wi-Fi. Or else some weird power outage. Every time she clicked on the image of the packet, which she had scanned in using her printer, as soon as it would start to download information and the little hourglass was flipping round and round, the computer crashed. Nothing but a black screen. After three tries, worried for the health of her laptop, Sheryl shut it down. She went into the other room and flipped a light switch. Lights came on just fine. She turned and looked back at her laptop. It felt hot to the touch. Best to leave it unplugged. Let it cool down.

The following day, Sheryl carried her tools and mystery seed packet over to her vegetable patch. She set it all carefully on the lawn, not hearing the hiss as the packet touched the wet grass because she was already focused on where she wanted to plant what might be an heirloom cultivar of zucchini. Jake was at school. He wouldn't be here for another hour.

"Who knows how old these are," she mused, "but it can't hurt to plant them." She chuckled. "If

they are overly abundant, I'll do 'drive-by squashing' of my new neighbors, all unlocked doors and vehicles fair game for them to discover a slumbering green lummox on a back porch or seat."

She'd shown Jake the packet but hesitated when he reached his hand for it. Stuck it in her pocket and brushed off her hands. Jake watched her, curious as to what that packet was and why she was so possessive of it. He was too polite to ask.

Sheryl knelt, her denim jeans soaking into the rich loam. *Like praying,* she caught herself thinking, *planting a garden is a form of prayer. The only problem: best be careful and know to whom and for what you pray.*

Soon three mounds or hills, as gardeners call them, were rowed in the watery sunshine and she stuck a finger deep into the top of each one. Reached behind her for the packet of old seeds and sprinkled them onto her sweat-stained palm. It stung. *Silly,* she thought, rubbing a finger across the skin. *Seeds don't sting. Must be a dust allergy or something from all that debris in the barn.*

In the next few minutes, each mound received its offering. She patted earth over the tops, stuffing the crumpled packet into a back pocket of her jeans. She staked the fencing back in place and walked to the house just as Jake pedaled up the driveway.

Since she met Jake, Sheryl had felt an awakening of poetry in her heart again. Perhaps through his enthusiasm, he would become her muse. In the next days, much to her surprise, she began to formulate more new poems in her head and later stopped to jot lines in a notebook. The first new work since her husband's death. She started to assemble a

manuscript and on the dedication page typed simply.
"For Jake, with love."

A Meeting of Poets

"Hey." She started up the porch steps. "How about some lemonades? I was just going to take a break," she gestured down at her muddy knees and laughed. "After, we can tackle the broken farm implements in the hay mow, if you're up for it."

Jake nodded. "Sure, no problem. A sip of lemonade would taste great after my bike ride." He watched her wash her hands at the kitchen sink while he petted Maggie. Sheryl always dabbed a small drop of perfume on each wrist after she did this. She claimed it repelled mosquitoes. It smelled musky and intense and Jake often imagined he could still smell it in the evening as he lay in bed.

Shortly they were seated in the soggy garden chairs, Maggie snuffling in the bushes along the edge of the woods, hoping for something to chase or eat. She had lost interest in them once she determined there was only lemonade and not any cookies.

"Say, you mentioned poetry the day we met, remember?" said Sheryl.

"Uh-huh." Jake blushed.

"So you write it, you said, yeah?"

"Uh-huh."

"Well, unless you are perusing some rare form of extremely short Japanese-form poetry limited to two syllables, you got any in your phone you could read to me?" She smiled and took a swallow of her drink.

He couldn't help staring as the smooth muscles of her throat worked. His eye followed down to the collar of her shirt. He looked up, abruptly red to the hair roots wishing the ground would just open up. Then he realized she had made a little joke at his expense but it wasn't mean, it was actually kinda cool because most people wouldn't even know what Japanese forms of poetry were.

"Yes, no, yeah, I mean yeah, I do have poems. I don't keep them in my phone though." He scooted forward in his seat so that he could reach into the back pocket of his battered Levi's. She saw he held a thick folded square of notebook papers which he unfolded with the care of a new parent swaddling an infant.

She smiled, remembering that thing that had happened in her solar plexus when the poetry woke up in her for the first time. She had been just about this age. She wondered if hormones had anything to do with it. Like being a chemical conduit or something. Of course, once the Muse spoke to you, that was it, 'til death do you part and all of that.

"I haven't been writing very long," he explained. "My English teacher had us do a unit on poetry. We had to search for poems and make a notebook and later we did a reading from a couple books in the school library. Finally, we had to write one. Lots of the kids hated it. I felt like… like I had a language to say

something I didn't know I needed." His voice trailed off.

She nodded. "I know exactly what you mean. So, you feel like reading aloud or you want me to read it? That is, of course, if you want to share your work with me."

"Oh yes, I do. I will. I've read yours, you know." He blurted this last part out and smacked himself lightly on the thigh.

"You have?" Sheryl was surprised. It had been so long since she had submitted or published any serious poetry. "You mean besides the TV jingle for that laundry detergent, that little song that turns into an ear worm?"

"Yes. I googled you. I went on Amazon, too. I got one of your books…" Then the jingle comment penetrated his consciousness: "What?"

"Oh? I, well, ha ha, I was a writer for an ad agency. Back in NYC. Long time ago I wrote that."

Jake scratched his head trying to think of TV commercials. "You wrote that?"

"Unfortunately, I did. Don't go blabbing to anyone. I am just relieved that phase of my life is past. It paid the bills after my husband died, but I wasn't happy."

Wow, he thought. *She was married*. He sighed.

"So read, will ya?" She wiggled into her chair to get comfortable. The ice cubes in her glass tinkled. Maggie flopped onto the grass at their feet. The freshly dug vegetable patch lay full of promise to the left of their chairs.

Jake paged through his now-unfolded collection. Suddenly he felt like every word he'd ever written

was stupid and worthless. He glanced at her. She smiled. He cleared his throat. She reached over and gently extracted one paper from his sheaf.

"Here, whatever is on here. Read me this poem."

So, he took a deep breath of her fragrance and started to read. Once he began, he forgot where he was or that he was reading to someone who was pretty much his idol. He succumbed to the magic, and the words wove a glittering net that eased his heart and lifted his spirits. As she listened and watched, her eyes half-closed, his face relaxed, and he gave himself over completely to the Muse. When the last word still echoed, almost a visible sparkle in the air between them, Sheryl sighed with pleasure.

"Jake, that was really good. It transported me to the place you were describing and made me feel such a longing. Would you read me another one?" She watched the blush creep up from his neck again. He was smiling as he nodded, though.

In the next weeks, they began a ritual of sharing a drink or treat outside in the sun by the vegetable garden if it was nice, in her kitchen at the table if not, followed by poems. He brought her chapbook, *Transplanted*, with him one day and asked her to sign and read from it. She inscribed it for him feeling obscurely flattered as tears pricked her eyelids. They became true friends.

After Planting

In the kitchen, the dog and cat milled around her feet, Maggie whining softly in her throat, whipping her tail against the lower cupboards. Sheryl's boots flopped on the mat by the back door, her muddied jeans a pile in front of the washer-dryer and she stood in underpants and sweatshirt scrubbing her hands at the sink. She held them close to her face in the bright light of the ceiling fixture to inspect for bites or rashes because no matter how much she scrubbed, they still stung. Nothing to see. Except her skin had taken on a faint greenish tinge which she attributed to the flickering fluorescent bulbs. She made a mental note to add new light bulbs to her hardware store list.

The phone rang. When she first arrived, she had gotten a contract with a new cell company and a whole new number. In the following weeks since, the phone had never rung, so she decided she must've been lucky enough to get a brand-new number. She looked at the caller ID. *Out of area.*

"Ha." She blew air out from compressed lips as she flipped the phone onto the table. After her mom's death, the only phone calls she did receive were

telemarketers, campaign fundraisers, and scams. She missed Lana. They used to talk for hours at least once a week. Some days she thought about taking the phone off her plan altogether and simply having Wi-Fi. When she turned to pick up her dirty jeans to put them in the washer, she caught Maggie dragging them by the pocket toward the back door.

"Maggie!" she shouted. Maggie stopped, looking embarrassed. "Give me back my jeans!" She pulled at the jeans, and for a moment, the dog refused to release her teeth. Sheryl swore she heard a low growl.

"Maggie, stop that!" Maggie dipped her head and opened her mouth. The pants fell to the floor. The pocket where the seed packet had been was soaked through. Maggie coughed and gagged. She trundled to her water dish and drank. Dripping jowls, she flopped down on her dog bed with an audible groan.

It was late afternoon, Jake long gone, and time for Maggie's chow. The sound of kibbles bouncing into a big metal bowl drifted out the open kitchen window. Someone could've heard it if a person were standing in the vegetable garden. The cat, Girlie, watched the garden from a windowsill. Her pupils dilated and her claws sank into the soft old wood of the window frame as she stared at something out there.

In the Garden

Prior to the day Sheryl had enlarged her veggie patch to include the three mounds of squash, seedlings had sprouted vigorously in her garden. Already the Early Girl tomato plant was loaded with buds. Cilantro with so many white flowers it reminded her of a bridal veil. Buds topped both oregano and basil, and the spinach had blown in spite of her repeated pinching off of the flower heads.

A row of mixed colors of leaf lettuces danced with frilled petticoats. The Kennebec potatoes burst through another section, relatives of the deadly nightshade vine. Acorn squash, cucumbers, and carving pumpkins meandered across the soil, winding graspers seeking the trellises or fencing that the gardener provided. Now, in the midst of all this riot of healthy life, three black humps filled out the remainder of the patch.

Full moonlight had shone bright white all night. As the sun rose, Sheryl no longer could see the faint face of the moon for the sunlight brightened and blanked it out, though she had often read in garden journals planting during a full moon was ideal. Later,

when the moon was taking the sky back, Sheryl prepared to go up to her bedroom to watch Netflix -- *Last Tango in Halifax,* with Maggie and Girlie piled next to her. She watched the evening news with her supper, first on cable then on PBS and found it the usual disgusting mixture of politics and violence.

Maggie and Girlie were the dinner clean-up crew, each licking a plate or utensil for whatever morsels remained of Sheryl's supper. They did not care if it was salad dressing or spaghetti sauce. It was always a treat. She knew many people frowned on giving pets human food and for that matter, having pets in bed, but she thought, *Tough you-know-what. My guys aren't fat and they love their treats.*

She petted each of them and gathered the dishes to load into the dishwasher. She filled the coffee maker with grounds so that when she stumbled down in the morning half-asleep, all she had to do was heat the water while she walked with Maggie on her first trip outside.

As she turned off the last living room lamp and checked that all the windows were locked, she looked into the yard hoping to see fireflies. It was the end of June, right about the time they should show up. The rising moon created black shadows across the lawn, elongated scary Halloween trees and other familiar objects turned strange as if under a spell in a not-so-nice fairytale.

For a second, she tried to make out where the vegetables were. She could barely make out the chairs and table where they sat during their poetry reading. A yearning pulled at her midsection, almost like the way it felt when a poem started, almost like desire, to

run out the door barefoot and to bury her face in the leaves of her vegetables. But she turned away from the windows and ignored it. A handful of color-changing solar lights she had stuck in the side yard went through their changes, blue, purple, red, green, gold and back. They had always fascinated her. The mathematical law of synchronicity applied here because sooner or later, the six solar lights worked in unison.

And again, from her upstairs writing studio, she glanced out the window with thoughts of the garden pricking her mind, but then the soundtrack of her show in the other room distracted her. Click of the studio light switch was so loud it echoed outside. She carried the folder with its sheaf of new "Jake Era" poems into her bedroom meaning to revise some.

Netflix flickered from the screen of her laptop. Sheryl had lit no lamp. Soon, the only sounds besides the show were a soft snore from Maggie and Sheryl's quiet breathing. Eventually the laptop asked her as it did every night, *Are you still there? If so, hit resume.* And since she was asleep, it silently turned itself off.

Girlie

Almost since kittenhood, it had been Girlie's habit to sit by Sheryl's head until she lifted the covers. Girlie would crawl under and have a good wash, then she curled up on Sheryl's chest and the two fell asleep this way. Cats have excellent hearing, in some ways better than dogs. When they lived in the city, Girlie often had a headache from the cacophony of noise that surrounded them 24-7. Here it was so silent she could hear owls' wings as the birds hunted in the woods. When she went into the basement and sat very still, she listened to mice scrambling twelve inches below the dirt floor and high up in the walls. She could also hear Sheryl's heart.

Girlie remembered from kittenhood the sound of her littermates' and her mother's hearts ticking and purring. That was why she liked to sleep on her human's chest. When she had first come to live with Sheryl and was sad because she missed her brothers and sisters, Sheryl wore a special sweatshirt with a pocket in front so that the kitten was always close to her chest. It helped Girlie get over her sadness.

These days, since Sheryl had discovered

whatever-it-was that she discovered in the barn and had worked planting in her garden, Girlie noticed a change had come over her human. Her heart no longer ticked smoothly whether fast or slow. Now it stuttered and paused. Girlie, afraid that it would stop in her sleep, gently dug her claws into Sheryl's skin.

Sometimes that prick roused her half out of sleep, and she would move and settle and the heartbeat would even out. Other times, when she was too deep in the dreamworld, Girlie washed her chin hard. She recalled her own mother doing this for many reasons when she was tiny. Sometimes she was able to wake Sheryl and often in the morning she sat quietly at her feet while she exclaimed and wondered over the bruise on her chin in the bathroom mirror.

Her eyes dark with worry, Girlie wondered at the bad thing that was happening. She knew Maggie was also aware of it. Suppose she was not able to wake Sheryl? How to keep a heart beating? She hunched herself into a fluffy ball on the windowsill and sighed.

Sheryl had felt the odd flutters in her heart. She knew she was of an age that she ought to get it checked out. Add to the list: find a new doctor.

Early Summer

The next June days passed in a flurry of springtime activity. Trying to get the lawn mowed in between thunderstorms (a challenge for Jake) and endless errands. Sheryl's attempts to write sitting at her laptop, gazing into nothingness, less frequent. Morning was her writing time. Sheryl found her thoughts always went back to the vegetable patch. She had a strange feeling some battle was going to take place. *Battle over what*, she thought as she opened her laptop to a new Microsoft Word file and typed a line of a poem. She felt like she was fighting for each word, and the harder that fight, the more urgent the feeling that those words must be written – and soon.

Years ago, when she was married, her husband was a fine chef and together they explored many nationalities of cuisine, cooking their way through long dark winters and reveling in a shared passion for tasty meals. She had always said a person could live an entire long lifespan and never eat the same thing twice if you really applied yourself and studied the cuisines of the world.

One particular winter they had decided on an

informal study of the meat pastry. There were beef wellington, pot pies, wontons... Polish potato meat pastries, knishes... every country, it seemed, had some version of some kind of meat wrapped in a succulent pastry. Her favorite was the empanada and the recipe they found in the *Joy of Cooking* with potatoes, crumbly beef, herbs and spices, wrapped in fragile melt-in-your-mouth pastry then baked. Served with a horseradish sauce that bit the tongue.

She sighed. Her mind came back to the present. The thought of horseradish reminded her she had forgotten to check the transplants she'd bought. She had dug one in by the back door and the other in a large open space near the barn. She remembered the autumn they had decided to dig horseradish roots at her old house. Unsuspecting and naïve, they tried to grind them in the kitchen and soon, with streaming eyes and noses and all the windows open to the north wind, learned that the next year they would set up the blender on the picnic table outside.

Good times. Her husband was gone. They'd met over a shared love of poetry, his of reading it, hers of writing it. He became the first adult family member in her life to support her dream of becoming a writer.

Shortly before his death he had asked her to "make it as a poet while I am still alive. I want to know you've achieved your dream." By some miracle, she had been in the right place at the right time to connect with a small publisher and ultimately to gift her husband the small poetry collection, dedicated to him. He had bought their first laptop and spent one winter cataloguing all her poems in it.

Her fingers lay idle on the keyboard, Maggie

snoring against her feet. Sheryl slapped the laptop shut. She grabbed the budding manuscript and carried it downstairs to set on the kitchen counter by the sink where she kept her little bottle of patchouli oil. She opened it, sniffed, and dabbed some on each wrist. With urgent thoughts of Jake running through her mind, she set the bottle on top of the folder. *If something ever happens to me, he will know to find it here.*

"C'mon, Mags. Let's go outside," she said aloud.

The dog roused with joy at that magic word, "outside" and clattered downstairs. Sheryl grabbed the leash and together they almost bounded into the yard. Maggie peed by a hydrangea bush and then found scents of rabbit, squirrel, and other visitors to sniff and ponder over. She also nipped every dandelion she found as if they were treats. Laughing Sheryl tousled Maggie's head. "That's one way to keep them in check."

They meandered around the big old house, Sheryl stopping now and then to pluck a weed from flowers or to snap a photo with her iPhone of some blossom or other. Eventually they found themselves at the vegetable garden. Among the favorites Sheryl and her husband used to cook in summer was stuffed squash blossoms. She salivated thinking of the mozzarella stuffed delicacies, fried in hot oil and served with salsa. She hoped the mystery seeds had quickened and would offer blossoms for this summer's delicacy. Chocolate chip zucchini bread was another delight.

Don had pulled in to chat while on his route the other day and mentioned a county fair was coming up that included a baking competition. Sheryl thought

maybe she would enter her chocolate chip zucchini bread. She signed up at Tom's Farm & Garden on a sheet on the community bulletin board and noted the list of names. Nobody she knew really, except some by sight, but it would be a good group to compete against. She decided Don and Jake could be her guinea pigs. They were both more than willing to struggle through loaves of the stuff if necessary.

With feet suddenly dug in, the dog refused to budge. Exasperated, Sheryl stepped over her and undid the clasp of the orange vegetable fence. She stopped short. "Huh," expelled from her lungs in a whoosh of air. Something was... different. The zucchini hills were no longer rounded and neat, but bumpy as if unseen lumps lurked beneath the surface. The adjacent tomatoes and other plants sagged, leaves drooping like wet laundry. Sheryl pushed aside some foliage to see if she could figure out what was going on by reaching for the base of a tomato plant. There. The main stalk was streaked with black. She snapped a shot of it with her phone and decided to run down to Tom's to see if the guys there would have any suggestions on how to combat it. She had been so looking forward to her tomatoes.

Researching the Mystery Fungus

"C'mon, Mags, bye bye in the car." Another favorite phrase of Maggie's. She galloped to the car, leaping in like a puppy. Sheryl lowered a back window so the dog could catch fragrances as they drove.

Both Tom, who owned the farm and garden supply store, which even carried some tanks of tropical and pond fish, and his co-worker were unsure what her photograph showed. But seeing as how it had been an unusually wet and cool summer so far, decided it was either some kind of fungus or rot, possibly an insect that loved wetness and burrowed up the stalks of plants. Loaded down with bottles and boxes of chemicals and fertilizers, with injunctions to make sure any pets stayed well away from the garden while these were applied,

"Don't worry," Sheryl assured them, "Maggie doesn't like my vegetable garden." She returned to the car.

Instead of going back home, Sheryl and Maggie

drove a fifteen-minute trip east to the nearest Walmart. She had decided to buy a couple of loaf pans and any other baking supplies and tools she needed after unpacking her kitchen boxes. It was cool enough for Maggie to be safe in the car, but Sheryl rolled the windows of the back seat of the Cherokee halfway down anyway. There was always a concern of some idiot trying to reach in. People got bitten that way because a lot of dogs consider the car their territory. Maggie wasn't a biter though.

When Sheryl trundled the cart back to the Jeep, she smiled at Maggie. That big black block of a head poked out the window, the constant smile and drool. "I didn't forget you, baby girl."

Sheryl rooted through a bag and ripped the cardboard and plastic off a thick chew bone, real bone stuffed with peanut butter. Maggie settled down in the back seat to enjoy her prize.

Sheryl Asks Jake

Nothing Sheryl tried seemed to help the failing plants. The zucchini mounds had broken open to reveal especially green pairs of dicotyledons. She hoped they would not be damaged by whatever infested the rest. They emanated an exotic beauty. She spent lost minutes any time she walked past, staring in rapture. The following day when Jake rolled up the driveway after school, she greeted him at the door with a frown.

"Hi. Come with me," she said, pulling the doorknob to make sure the old door latched. Sometimes she found Girlie pressing paws against the screen and didn't want her lost outside.

Jake dropped his pack on a lawn chair and followed Sheryl around the back of the house. Maggie swirled between his legs threatening to knock him down in her exuberance at the sight of her friend. Sheryl had stopped next to the vegetable garden and pointed at it. She turned to say something to the boy as he walked up beside her and squatted to better pet Maggie.

"See that?" she demanded rather harshly. Then,

"Sorry," she muttered at the sight of his startled expression from her tone.

Jake stood up and bent down over the rows of vegetable plants. He noticed the squash hills. "Oh, you added some squash or pumpkins?" he asked.

"Uh huh. But look at the other drooping plants. Something is damaging my garden. I went to town. Talked to the guys at Tom's, and they sent me home with tons of stuff, but nothing seems to help. I am worried the squash will be infected too."

Jake looked more closely. He took a tomato seedling gently between his fingers. Beneath the limp leaves, the stalk showed black streaks. He checked each lettuce, every pepper, but when he reached for the zucchinis, Sheryl jerked him back by his jacket hem, "Don't touch those!"

He backed up a step looking for the dog. She was up on the porch sitting on the door mat, frowning in anxiety in their direction.

"I see what you mean. I don't know what that could be. Did you take a picture with your phone to show those guys?"

She nodded.

Jake was at a loss. He didn't know why she was so agitated about dying plants. Those could easily be replaced. It was still early enough in the season.

They worked a short while organizing junk in the barn and then sat for a minute. "Hey, I have an idea," Jake said. "Jorge and I go to Brookline on the weekends after work. We take the bus for a class at the community college."

"Oh?" said Sheryl, not paying too much

attention. Her mind was on her squash seedlings. She raked her fingers through her hair.

"When we get done this Saturday afternoon, we can maybe go to the library. They have a big ass — oops big computer there. I will see if I can do some research. They have the whole horticulture program at the college too. If anybody can help, it'll be those plant geeks."

At this, she did chuckle. "Who are you calling a 'geek,' poetry nerd." They laughed together.

He loved the fragrance of her perfume. When he tried to return an old sweatshirt she'd said had been her husband's, borrowed after a sudden rainstorm last week, she said he should keep it or donate it, but instead he kept it under his pillow. It smelled like that scent of perfume and cigarette smoke that, to his heart, said simply: *Sheryl*.

Trying hard not to think of this in front of her, he hugged Maggie goodbye and jumped on his bike.

Jake and Jorge's Research Adventure: A Bus Ride to the College

Saturday afternoon the boys went to their class and as promised, meandered their way to the library while pausing to gawk at the hot college chicks crossing campus. One especially beautiful blonde coed smirked, "Dream on, boys," as she swept by in a cloud of Herbal Essence shampoo. That was embarrassing.

After a brief bout of punching each other in the arms, the boys trotted up the steps and soon were ensconced at a big table with their books spread out in front of a computer terminal.

Jorge's cousin was a student here and had let them borrow his ID card. You had to have it to access the computer lab. They hoped hoodies and sunglasses disguised their age. But then, nobody was really paying attention to them.

They came up empty on plant ID with the library computer, so Jake asked the young woman at the desk for permission to go into the microfiche room. Once

settled there, scrolling, scrolling suddenly Jake gasped. Jorge leaned in.

"Check this out! It's that plant! It's a really ancient strain of squash, distantly related to wild zucchini. Someone brought it from somewhere in middle Europe like Slovakia a hundred years ago or more... And look down here, it's gorgeous. Check out those flowers — they smell like rotten meat and the sap is toxic. It emits a neurotoxin." He scrolled some more. "And here it says it only blooms during the full moon. Prefers to be planted during a blood moon." Their eyebrows raised. Jake continued scrolling.

"It sure is beautiful!"

The micro-fiche machine clicked. "And it is so rare, it's protected." They look at each other. "So, nobody is gonna pull it or torch it."

"Check out these photos. These are weird, they're all pictures of murder scenes. Look, says in this one a seven-year-old girl went missing and was never found. Look in the background — see that leaf? It's the same plant. And in this old clipping — story about somebody's dog getting lost and only the collar was left, see? There is a section of vine — it's the same plant!"

"Whoa, creepy, dude!"

"The name, what is it called? *Medusa oblongata.* Isn't that the name of that goddess with the snake hair? She turned people to stone with one look?"

"Yeah."

They scrolled further and came to a list of regional folklore sources.

"According to legend this plant is colloquially known as the 'man-eater.' It is said it has an ability to

lure an unsuspecting human to be its caregiver and when it has fruited and seeds are set, the old ones say the man-eater kills the host and consumes him or her."

They looked at each other. "You don't think that's real, do you?"

"I don't know what to think. Something is definitely off about that set of plants and the seed packet Sheryl found. Ever since she planted them, she has definitely started to act weird. Like especially around the garden. Once I was starting to recite a stanza of a poem to her and she almost shoved me around the side yard and away from the garden. When I asked her why, she pointed to the plants. The leaves were droopy. But it was hot and sunny so who cared? It happens. *She* cared that's for sure, so we moved."

Jake's mom wanted them home by suppertime but as he surfaced from the screen, he saw that sun was descending outside. And the last bus left at five.

"C'mon, we'll miss the bus."

They shuffled everything into piles to cram into their packs as they ran for the bus stop. A lot of people were waiting. Someone said, "Bus is late."

Jake pulled out his phone to text his mom. At least it wasn't his fault. Finally, when the grumbling in the crowd had reached a certain loudness, the bus pulled in with the sign over the windscreen for Jake's town. People queued up and the boys fell in line. Slowly the line snaked onto the vehicle. It seemed to be filling up back to front — a bunch from the casino it sounded like — so Jorge snagged a seat just two rows behind the driver.

Someone else grumbled that the bus had been delayed because of construction and that the driver was new and had gotten lost. Just then the driver herself stepped up into the bus. Jake elbowed his friend.

"Shut your mouth, 'Mano," whispered Jorge. "You'll catch a fly."

She was easily six feet tall and her skin was the color of coffee swirled with just a hint of milk. She filled out her crisp uniform with muscle. When she opened her mouth to speak—she apologized to the riders for the lateness—one gold front tooth gleamed in the gathering dusk.

She wore her hair straight and short and a pair of simple gold earrings matched the gold insignia on her collar points and her tie tack. She swung into her seat, stowed her briefcase between seat and wall and snapped on her belt. She picked up the dash mic and spoke into it. Before long, the bus grumbled as she shifted it into gear and pulled out.

Across the aisle from the boys sat a woman with one foot in a cast. Almost as soon as they hit the highway or even had started up the entrance ramp, the rowdiness began from way back in the bus. Jake and Jorge could hear it even with their ear buds in. Both boys turned their music off because it seemed important to hear what was happening. Overhead the driver's face looked inscrutable in the rearview mirror.

"The fuck they send a new driver for?" shouted someone in the way back.

"Yeah, one who got lost too," another loudly agreed.

She flicked the windshield wipers on during a brief cloud burst.

"Hell you goin', girl? I think we are *still* lost and you don't know what the fuck you're doing."

More voices joined in. Jake's mouth dried as his heart sped up. He wished the driver would do something but what, he didn't know. She looked like she might be in the army or something. No matter how rude the taunting went, she just drove. But more and more voices joined the hecklers.

Jorge whispered to Jake, "Remember when we were studying the Nazis in history and the teacher was talking about herd mentality?"

Jake recalled that all too well. The bus began to descend an off-ramp. He checked his phone. They'd only been on the road for about fifteen minutes. There was no stop yet.

"Fuck now you doing, girl? Maybe we should just take over and drive."

Looking out the window, Jake was sure he recognized some construction they'd passed going the other direction. The driver spoke into her mic too softly for the boys to hear around the plastic bullet proof partition that separated the driver from passengers. Jorge elbowed him and pointed. They both glanced behind but really could make out no particular person. Sure enough, the station that was next to the college campus came into sight.

"What's happening?" asked the little lady in the cast across the aisle.

The boys shrugged helplessly.

"I have to meet my friend at eight o'clock. She's eighty-two and has no cell phone. She won't know

where I am."

Yeah, nobody knows, thought Jake.

The driver slammed the bus into park and reached under her seat for the briefcase. She climbed out and turned to face the passengers.

"I, for sure, do not have to take this shit! You all can find another way home." And with that she descended the steps and walked into the station.

Jake and Jorge gaped at each other.

"I'm going in," said Jake to the lady in the cast. To Jorge, "Guard my shit."

He zipped down the steps — the door was locked in open position — and hurried into the bus depot. At once he saw the driver standing in a group of what looked like security guards. He edged closer hoping to eavesdrop. She saw him. "Go on back to your seat," she told him "Just sit tight. It'll be okay."

Reluctantly he climbed back into the bus. An aura of alcoholic fumes and rage emanated from the far end. He threw his body down next to his friend whose normally tan face was a pale blur. A couple cop cars zoomed into the parking area. The hecklers started crowing, "Oooh, somebody's in trouble!"

As he was about to tell Jorge what the driver had said to him, two of the biggest, tallest police he'd ever seen in real life stomped onto the bus. Followed by two more.

The jerk in back started to shout at the cops, "You oughtta arrest the driver!"

Instead, much to that person's shock, each bicep was gripped tight by an officer and the next thing she knew — it was a woman Jake saw — she was being forcibly lifted off the bus. Her friend was likewise

escorted into the station as well.

Time passed. The bus sat there. Nobody said a word. Jake's phone kept beeping—his mom sending frantic texts. He turned off the sound because he couldn't tell her anything anyway. The driver came out of the revolving door and hoisted herself back into the bus. One officer accompanied her. He looked at the passengers. "Anybody else got a problem?"

A meek chorus of "No, sirs" drifted up the aisle.

"Alright then. Have a good night and let this woman do her job." He left.

The bus engine growled to life and hand-over-hand she turned the steering wheel as she piloted them out of the lot. As soon as they were on the highway heading for home, Jake leaned forward. She glanced at him in the rear view.

"Thanks!" he said loudly. "Thank you for keeping us safe."

"Welcome." More voices joined Jake's.

After his mom had fed them a late dinner of fish sandwiches and fries, the boys lay in the darkness of Jake's room.

Jorge whispered, "That was so scary. How first it was one person, then two, then a whole bunch of them. Like, like..."

"A mutiny," Jake answered, "like pirates taking over a ship."

"She was so brave, that driver."

Jake pushed up on one elbow. "But what is scarier is that plant. What happened on the bus, how like one mood spread to lots of people and changed their behavior reminds me of the folk tale about that

plant getting somebody to take care of it. Look at all the information we found about it."

He climbed out of bed and grabbed his backpack. He pulled out stacks of print-outs—they'd emptied their pockets of coin at the copy machine—so they could study what they'd found.

Jorge crouched down next to him. He pointed at the murder photos, "Nothing good. You think a plant can be evil? You think a plant has awareness like can make itself so beautiful that someone can't resist it and then *chomp!* You gone!?"

Their eyes met in the half-light from the streetlamp outside. Was Sheryl in danger? And if so, how to let her know?

They finally fell asleep, but what dreams they had were troubled by taunting voices, vines that snaked across lawns to wrap around their ankles, vines that had impossibly beautiful flowers but stank of rotting meat.

In Sheryl's Garden

The zucchini was not infested. As the rest of the garden rotted and mildewed, their beauty grew with almost obscene vigor. The scent in the yard reminded Sheryl of a dead mouse decaying in a wall. The dog refused to go back there at all. Sheryl took disproportionate joy in the compelling beauty of the plants. Their creamy flowers were so stunning a person felt they must be protected at all costs. She had to squint when she looked at them. Sometimes she couldn't stop looking at them not even when her heart raced and skipped the closer she stood.

As the county fair date grew closer, she began to wonder if other competitors were perhaps sabotaging her garden. She started trying to stay awake all night, sitting in her studio window, watching over the vegetable garden. The idea of the squash plants being killed in addition to all the others terrified and angered her. She knew she wasn't popular in town and didn't really care. Small towns were kind of incestuous anyway.

All she wanted was time and space to write, though if she was brutally honest with herself, no

writing was happening. Well, some of the best poetry she'd ever written had started to accumulate in a folder on her desk but as time passed, every time she thought about a line or jotting something down, her heart skipped, and she felt too tired to bother. She pushed that thought aside as if it were a bothersome gnat and returned to obsessing about which of her neighbors was poisoning her garden.

When she did errands in town and talked to the postal clerk, she used to joke, "My zucchinis are taking over the world." At the drugstore, picking up her scrips, she'd said, "If I am ever MIA, come looking for me by the zucchini." *Ha ha.* Everyone knew how prolific they were. Some people told stories of leaving squash overflow in people's cars in the church parking lot on Sundays. Now she kept silent and stared at one person after another, wondering, *was this the culprit?* She debated telling Don during what had become his weekly visit. Often, he brought donuts.

If she shared this with the mailman, however, suppose he told whoever was doing it. No, she decided to keep her thoughts to herself. Everyone knew Don was a chatterbox anyway. Even if he was especially fond of animals and always brought them treats. Nope, she was not going to trust him with this.

Then her restless mind landed on Jake. He had ample opportunity to poison her plants. All his bullshit about research at the horticulture department at the college. Just crap. The past few weeks when they'd shared poetry in the garden, she felt very anxious. Was it her imagination or did the mystery vines seem to wither when voices read verse aloud?

She'd decided they should either read indoors only or move to the front yard.

She struggled to work on her new manuscript every morning, but it was more and more exhausting. She hadn't felt like chatting with him in a while, so she left notes stuck to the screen door with his list of chores. Once the thought of him hurting her garden woke, it took over her mind. She decided to fire him. Who knew what he had really been looking up that Saturday.

A Shocking Goodbye

Two days later, Jake rolled up the driveway and knocked on the door. She came out on the porch and quite curtly told him she no longer needed his help in the yard. She thrust cash at his hand "for the last week." He was confused, apologizing and stumbling over his words. "But I wanted to show you what we found out at the university... about your plants." He thrust a packet of printouts at her.

"Nope, thanks, I don't need any more help. We got the barn cleared out and the garden in. I can handle the lawn from now on."

She turned and went in without another word, slamming the door, which made Maggie bark inside, and then he could clearly hear the sound of the lock engaging.

His heart broke in a thousand pieces. She'd paid him but he didn't want that money, so he squeezed it between the doors and slowly walked down the porch steps.

For a few minutes, he stood there unable to bring himself to leave yet. Jake walked back up on the porch and found the door was now unlocked. He went

inside, catching sight of Sheryl through the kitchen window, in the side yard with an armload of books, tossing them one by one into a blaze.

He ran out to her. "What are you doing?!"

She jerked around. He noticed the title of what she was burning and reached to rescue the books from her hand. Poetry books! She is burning all her poetry books. She shoved him away again.

"Why are you burning all your poetry books?" he shouted. "Stop! You *love* poetry!"

A cloud of sparks floated skyward. "I'm done with poetry. It's stupid!! I'm sorry I ever started it with you. Go on, get out of here! Get a real job!"

He stood there, frozen for a moment, watching her as she dropped in more books, tore pages out and fed them to the flames. He was in shock. He went back into the kitchen and, on impulse, did something he would never have done otherwise. He saw a folder with the word "manuscript" on the counter underneath her little perfume bottle by the sink. He snatched it and shoved it beneath his jacket before she had a chance to come after him, leaving the pile of printouts on the counter. For good measure, he grabbed the patchouli bottle too and ran out the front door, down the steps.

He swung his leg over his bike and headed down the driveway. He stopped by the mailbox to check for traffic. Looking back over his shoulder, he could see he was out of sight of the house. He reached into his vest and pulled out a folded packet. Quickly, before he could change his mind, he slipped it into the mailbox. It contained several poems he had started since he had been coming to work with her.

One day, when they'd sat passing a smoke back and forth, him coughing because he was too embarrassed to admit he'd never tried one, Sheryl had shared one of her new poems aloud with him. He was so thrilled that she actually trusted him enough, he could barely remember what it was about when he laid in bed that night.

It didn't help that his boner distracted him. When she'd bend over, if he was in the right vantage point, he could see the swells of her breasts right down the middle of her shirt. Sometimes even a nipple, hard against the fabric. The scent of her.

Now as he rode away, tears dripped down his cheeks. Angrily he scrubbed them with the sleeve of his jacket. It was a trade he justified in his mind. He had her poems, he'd left her his in a spot he was pretty sure she wouldn't look anymore.

Plus, he left the research results. Maybe she would read them. Something had been bugging him for a while. He remembered the day she had asked him to carry their chairs to the front yard. "The sun's in my eyes," she'd said. Made no sense at the time, but he realized the move took them farther away from the garden. From that mystery plant. What did poetry have to do with the vine? He touched the stolen folder, safe under his jacket.

One evening, shortly after this event, at sunset Jake had ridden his bike out to her house. No lights were on. He hoped Maggie didn't hear him. Quietly he snuck around back. He had a strange theory as to why she'd moved their reading spot. He slipped a sheet of paper from his back pocket. He stood facing

the giant plants, a love poem he had written for her in his hands. In a quiet voice he began to read. The nearest leaf trembled. He read a few more lines, scrubbed his eyes. No mistake the plant reacted to the poem. It didn't like it.

Sheryl Ponders Garden Mysteries

From around the time since she had planted those antique seeds, Sheryl had been vaguely aware that while she found Japanese beetles on grape vines nearby and other insects, nothing living flew into her garden any more. Or if it did, it did not fly out. She wondered how the zucchini would be pollinated since bees fared no better. Maybe this ancient strain of squash was some sort of self-pollinator. There were no longer earthworms in the loam at the base of the plants. Just dark black soil that resembled coffee grounds.

Sheryl and Maggie had seen many rabbits hopping around since they moved here, squirrels that scuffled in the treetops, and chipmunks. They all avoided the vegetable area but liked to eat corn kernels that fell from the bird feeder. One day, she sat in her studio, not working, hands limp on the keyboard, staring out the window at the garden. She'd actually rearranged her office furniture so she could sit by the window to watch over it. She found

herself slightly anxious if she couldn't see the plants or if she stayed away from home too long.

July brought its summer delights: wild black raspberries, cherries, and countless flowers. Baby birds grew up and flew away and then the second clutch was hatched. Now parents spent time fattening on insects and seeds for winter and, for those that did it, migration.

Everything else in Sheryl's garden had long since died and shriveled to nothing. The zucchini were enormous. She had taken some photos, longing to post their pictures online somewhere, some plant forum or YouTube because she was sure these were record-breaking plants. Kind of amazing, wasn't it, that they'd survived for so long in a dusty box on a barn shelf? Who knew how old those seeds were.

Her paranoia grew that some person in the upcoming bake-off had deliberately poisoned her garden and just by a miracle, had managed not to kill the squash she planned to compete with. She chose not to post any photos because who knew who was watching, privacy settings be damned. She found the papers Jake had left for her and she threw them in the fire without reading.

Unable to resist the temptation for stuffed squash blossoms any longer and armed with a plastic freezer bag to collect them, one afternoon Sheryl went out to pick some. On the counter she had set up bowls of egg wash, flour, and the stuffing for them made of mixed cheeses, breadcrumbs, and herbs.

Girlie jumped on the drain board and stuck her head into the cheese bowl. Was good, but she didn't like any herb except catnip. Mags wagged nervously.

She knew cats were not supposed to be on the counter in the people food. Girlie just glared at her in a superior way and whisked past her, her tail an exclamation of "you are SUCH a baby!"

Stuffed Squash Blossoms

As soon as she touched the first male blossom, a tingle zapped Sheryl's arm. "Ow!" she shouted, pulling back, thinking a hornet had stung her. Nothing. She stepped into the barn to don a long-sleeved jacket and gardening gloves. Nothing was stopping her harvest of these long-awaited flowers.

She managed to grab a bagful with only a few nasty stings and scratches. When she glanced at herself in the bathroom mirror that night, under the greenish light of that fluorescent—note to self, buy more light bulbs—she was surprised at the number of scratches that covered her body. She turned this way and that, lifting her arms and legs trying to see the backs with a hand mirror. Odd to have so many of what looked like insect bites when so few insects inhabited her vegetable patch.

"I must be getting really forgetful and clumsy in my old age," she laughed at herself. "I better learn to climb over the garden fence more carefully."

The stuffed blossoms smelled delicious cooking, but the fragrance of cilantro and thyme was threaded through with a faint scent of rot. When they were a

perfect golden brown, she scooped them out of the pan and laid them on a bed of paper towels to soak up the excess oil. She recalled years past giving herself "pizza mouth" by eating too-hot blossoms and getting burnt by the melted cheese. She exhorted herself to *wait!*

She took a bite. Flavors flooded her senses along with memories of other summers. She chewed and swallowed. Felt a faint bit nauseous. She gobbled some more, slathered with salsa. The nausea must be from eating too fast. Lately it seemed she had forgotten to eat breakfast and lunch many days. She'd noticed a new gauntness around her face and ribs in the bathroom mirror.

As she chewed, she recalled noticing several fingerling zucchini squashes. She decided her next meal venture would include some of them, sliced thin and fried al dente. They were from the fertilized female flowers. Sad, there was usually a bevy of male flowers around one female, but the boys all died immediately after their job was done.

Her thoughts were interrupted by such a wave of nausea, she knocked her chair over racing for the toilet. She knelt there, saliva flooding her mouth, swallowing, swallowing. Maggie wagged worriedly in the doorway. Girlie regarded her from up on the sink. Eventually it passed and she eased back against the tub. A thought surfaced from the depths of her mind, *Something is wrong here. Something about those plants.* Immediately, she brushed the thought away.

Later that night, she sat in her window seat watching the garden in the moonlight. A rabbit nosed out from the hedgerow and hopped slowly into the

yard. While the wild animals, like her own, avoided the garden, this guy was intent on something and strayed closer and closer to the gigantic zucchini plants.

Suddenly a thin tendril of vine unraveled from a stalk of the plant and snapped across the grass as fast as a striking snake and wrapped itself around the rabbit before it knew what was going on.

Goosebumps rose all over Sheryl's skin at the quavering wail of the dying bunny. She shook her head, rubbed her eyes and stuck her fingers in her ears. Mags was barking, stumping from window to window, rearing up on her hind legs trying to see out. Sheryl stared down at the grass. Only a furrowed trail of rabbit paws clawing for safety, leading to the squash plant was shadowed in the moon's light.

No, she decided while she looked into her own eyes in the bathroom mirror. *That is NOT what I saw. I ate something, some herb probably that didn't agree with me and now I'm having hallucinations. God knows, I feel like I have the flu.* That had to be the reason her skin had taken such a greenish tinge. She recalled her mother using some expression when she was a kid like "he turned green around the gills" when someone was sick to their stomach.

The Gun

The next morning after a few sips of coffee and clad in a grimy sweatshirt, dirty jeans, and flip-flops, Sheryl jumped in the Jeep without Maggie, who stood on the living room couch gazing mournfully at the retreating vehicle. Dreams had troubled Sheryl's sleep of unseen assailants creeping in the shadows around her yard. She had decided to buy a gun.

At Walmart with her ball cap pulled low and her sunglasses on to hide her red-rimmed eyes, she approached the clerk in the firearm department. She wondered if you needed a license to buy a rifle.

"Help you, ma'am?" a middle-aged man with a belly and nose that suggested he liked his beer leaned on the glass counter over a display of boxes of ammunition.

"Yes, please. I'd like to buy a gun."

"Okay well, what sort of gun did you have in mind?"

She hesitated.

"What do you want to use it for?" he tried again. "Target practice? Deer hunting?"

"Oh." She shook herself. "I, I need it for uh,

varmints." She couldn't believe the word 'varmints' had just left her lips. The guy didn't seem fazed.

"Okay then, you got a problem with foxes or coyotes, you'll be wanting one of these babies." He took a .22 rifle bearing a lovely carved stock out of another case.

Sheryl felt bemused again at the word *lovely* crossing her mind in regard to a part of a firearm. He passed it across the counter to her. She smelled the gun oil as she stroked the wood. It was a new scent and she liked it. Experimentally, she lifted it to her shoulder then quickly put it down.

"I'll take it." She began to dig into her lumpy shoulder bag for a credit card.

"First, you have to fill out this paperwork. We run a background check, usually takes twenty-four to thirty-six hours for the national database to see if you've ever been arrested for violations." He passed the papers and a pen over to her.

She felt sick to her stomach. She wanted the rifle today, but Sheryl went ahead and filled in her name, address, and phone number.

The clerk continued, saying, "Then if it is all hunky dory, we'll give you a call and you can come pick up your rifle."

He suggested a copper jacketed type of ammunition that was better, in his opinion, than shotgun shells with their mess of pellets, and along with her copies of everything, included a gun safety training course flyer.

Three days later, this time both she and Maggie jumped into the Cherokee and Sheryl collected her gun and ammunition and a big bone (for Maggie), a

packet of catnip mice (for Girlie), and a box of Miracle Gro slow-release pelleted plant food (for the zucchini). It never crossed her mind to take the gun safety class. All she knew was that you had to tuck the stock tight into your shoulder and be prepared for the push of recoil. She had decided on a padded nylon waterproof gun case in forest green with a handy side pocket for ammo, gun cleaning tools, wallet, and so forth.

As she drove home, with Justin Bieber singing in Spanish on the radio and Maggie chomping in the back seat, her feelings of nausea and anxiety receded. Getting a rifle was the right thing to do.

In the days that followed, Maggie barked ferociously every time Sheryl went to work in the garden. She finally locked the old dog in the bathroom. As for her inclinations to write or to eat or do errands, nothing seemed to matter but tending the garden. She did manage to harvest some more blossoms and even wrestled a small squash off a tough vine to eat. Each time, they nauseated her.

During the next full moon cycle, she started going out to work in the garden in the moonlight. On the rare occasions that she dozed off, her dreams were full of lustful fantasies of running naked in the darkness into the vegetable patch and wrapping her body with stinging zucchini leaves. Of stroking a long turgid squash and rubbing it against her female parts. Of looking down at her naked body and seeing her skin had turned electric green.

One morning she startled awake with the rifle lying under the sheet next to her like a lover. She had no memory of putting it there. A few days later, when

she jolted awake at 2 am in the chair she'd dragged to the studio window to guard the garden, her forehead ached. Something crashed to the floor as she scrabbled for the light switch. She regarded herself in the cloudy mirror, a grooved circle the size of a quarter dented deep into the skin at the center of her forehead. It was angry purplish-green. She stumbled back into her study and found the .22 lying on the floor in front of her chair. She must have fallen forward where she sat, asleep with her head propped on the muzzle of the firearm. She was appalled to find the trigger guard wet with sweat. Guns had to stay dry. She looked at her hands. They smelled of oil.

The sun was just peeking over the trees, so she decided the night was done. Carefully she laid the rifle into its case, zipped that and put it on the top shelf of her closet for the day. Once she would've asked Don, who was a veteran of Afghanistan and had some medals, to show her how to use it. But now she didn't want him to know she had the rifle. It was her secret to be guarded as carefully as the garden.

She was glad she'd fired Jake. One less snoop coming around. Briefly the memory of a manuscript crossed her mind, something precious she had discovered inside herself after such a long time. Uneasiness followed. Maybe she should burn that, too. Yes. But no matter how frantically she searched the house, she could not find that folder of new poems.

Sometimes in her restless sleeps she'd dream of a boy toasting marshmallows with her and sharing his poetry but she could never recall them once she woke up. Her cheeks were often wet after.

Obsessed or Possessed?

Summer days ambled past; she became more obsessed with the garden to the exclusion of everything else. Instead of feeding Maggie and Girlie, she left their bags of chow in the open pantry door and let them graze as they needed. Sometimes she took Maggie outside. Sometimes she forgot. Her kitchen counter was strewn with baking paraphernalia, flour spilled all over with cat paw prints through it, cans of baking soda, oily measuring cups, a bag of chocolate chips well within Maggie's reach even though Sheryl had once known that chocolate was bad for dogs.

She forgot to fill their water bowls, but the toilet lid was up, so for as long as that water lasted, they had something to drink. She had to get out to the garden. She had zucchini to pick.

One day, Don, who was the only regular visitor to Sheryl's house, had a certified letter she needed to sign for.

Maggie and Girlie are Afraid

Ever since the last trip to Walmart, Maggie had become increasingly afraid. Her woman wasn't acting right. She smelled of something all dogs were born knowing never to eat. She never spent time petting her anymore and Maggie's summer fur-shed was making painful mats, especially in her arm pits. She chewed at herself trying to bite them off. Sheryl would shout at her, "Stop that goddamn chewing!!" Maggie wasn't clear what the words meant, but the tone and a book hurled in her direction were easy to understand – and hurt.

She wished the boy with the gentle hands still came, but he hadn't been to visit in so long there was no smell of him anywhere in the house, not even the chair in the living room where he would sit sometimes. Maggie sniffed it sadly.

Girlie fared no better. The two animals had given up sleeping with Sheryl. Her thrashing legs booted them off the bed more nights than not. For another, that smell. The last few times Girlie had managed to stay on Sheryl's chest at night, after licking the strange smelling sweat off her chin, the cat would have to find

a rug and vomit. Only greenish juice came up, but when Maggie found it, she'd nosed at the rug until a corner came up and covered it.

The last straw was the appearance of the weapon next to her under the sheets. The animals left her alone with it. She carried the rifle with her everywhere from bed to garden and back. Propped it against the door frame in the kitchen or laid it across her lap in the studio as she sat night after night by the window mesmerized by the scene outside while the zucchini climbed higher and higher.

Some nights Sheryl swore she could hear a song coming from it, a high-pitched, cicada-like vibration. It called to her and filled her with a longing so intense it made her stomach cramp and the crotch of her underwear damp. Soon she dragged a blanket and pillow outside, along with the gun, and slept stretched alongside the vegetable garden. Any intruders would have to step on her.

Intruders were a flimsy excuse. She couldn't bear to be away from her exuberant, gorgeous squash plants.

The animals slept in Maggie's basket in the kitchen, Girlie a hump on Maggie's flank, the dog's tail covering her nose.

Don's Surprise

Don parked his rusty mail truck in the driveway and wrestled the envelope out of the back. It was his half-day, Saturday, early August. Cicadas were hatched and singing, a sure sign summer was passing. The house, which he knew she had bought to renovate, looked strangely neglected. Flower beds had not been weeded. Portulaca was being choked out by purslane. Geraniums drowned in boxes overflowing with rainwater. Morning glories in pots along the porch rail withered for lack of it. A single boot lay on its side on a mat by the front door, a pair of dirty gardening jeans cast off on the bench above it.

Jake had stopped by his house a few weeks ago, dejected. Turned out she had told him she no longer needed his help. The boy hadn't stayed long, but spilled his guts while he was there.

When he raised his hand to knock on the front door, it squeaked open, fetching up against something. Don poked his head around the door. Tipped over boxes, spilled papers, and other junk lay on the foyer mat, the funny one he liked that had paw prints painted on and said *Wipe Your Paws*.

Something smelled bad, too.

"Hello?" he called. "Anyone home?"

Just then a black shape blasted out of a corner and almost knocked him down. He had the impression of teeth and claws and then realized, this was Sheryl's old dog. "Maggie!" He gathered the shivering beast to his chest, talking soft to her, petting her rough fur. "It's alright girl. I got you now. Where is your mama, hmm?"

She whimpered and groaned with relief. Then she bolted down the porch steps and ran to his mail truck. He'd left the door open and in she hopped just as Sheryl had predicted the first time Don had stopped by and given the pets treats.

He got to his feet and walked toward the kitchen. The pantry closet stood open, a large bag of dog food pulled out and mostly eaten. The toilet lid was up in the bathroom and the water dry. What had happened here? Then the cat jumped onto his shoulders from where she was hiding on the landing. He screamed. She dug her claws in.

"Hey, Girlie-girl. Don is here. It's okay. We're gonna find your mama. Maybe she got sick and needs help, huh?" Girlie butted his face hard with her head.

He walked through the downstairs carrying the cat. There was dog poop in a corner with old papers and rug nosed up as if in embarrassment to cover it. He found the cat box overflowing in the kitchen and a bag of food pulled from a counter cabinet, clawed open for Girlie to have eaten from it.

He wandered through the kitchen, opened the door to the garage. The Cherokee was there. Windshield had a thin layer of dust on it. He drew a

finger through it. He spied a cat carrier up on a shelf and made a snap decision. Sure, if she turned up, he would just explain he'd felt something was amiss and had taken the animals home to watch over until her return. She knew they liked him from his many visits. The cat clung to his shirt for a moment then allowed herself to be put into her crate.

Carrying this in one hand, he walked through the rest of the house. Everything was neglected. Dishes piled in the sink. Coffee pot moldy. Upstairs he saw her study the desk with her abandoned laptop. He checked it. Battery dead. A chair leaned against the wall under the window. Looked as if someone sat there often looking at… what? A dirty tee shirt and bra lay slumped in a pile by the chair legs.

His eyes traveled out and down to the garden below. The squash plants were almost touching the second story window frames! He rubbed his eyes, thinking he was having a stroke or maybe an episode of PTSD. But no, enormous leaves rustled against the shingles, uttering little whispers that seemed to beg him to let them come inside. His heart pounded in his ears.

"What the hell?" he muttered.

To Meet a Monster

He stumbled downstairs as fast as he could, his mailbag smacking into his thigh. He set Girlie's crate in the truck beside Maggie and ran around the back of the house to the garden. The very air seemed to pulsate with these giant plants. The smell made him bend over to gag and cough. He lost his breakfast donut and black coffee, splattering the ground between his knees and his pants' cuffs. That stench!

He grappled in his back pocket for the large handkerchief he kept there as he rubbed one wrist across his mouth. He tied it around his face like a bandit in a cowboy movie. Even with his nose and mouth covered, the smell made his eyes water. He wasn't even sure if he was done vomiting.

As he edged carefully closer, mindful of... who knew what, images of being dragged screaming under a zucchini leaf by a tendril the thickness of a rope racing through his head, he saw something that made his heart stutter and skip, Sheryl's other boot. Just one lonely boot, tipped over at the edge of a cedar plank. Next to it leaned a shiny new .22 with an intricately carved stock.

"What the hell was she doing with a gun?" he asked out loud. He picked it up carefully, checking to be sure the safety was on.

Dashing to the edge of the yard to find a branch, because he had a strong aversion to touching the leaves, Don crept back and slipped the tip of it beneath some of the tarp-sized leaves not too far from where the boot lay.

The humming sound intensified. It reminded him of the hornet nest he'd stumbled on by accident as a kid. Those really mean black ones with the white faces that burrowed in the ground. Nothing fazed them.

Underneath the leaf, he saw a scrap of a torn, bloody blanket and a pillow. He dropped the maple branch, but clung to the rifle, and began to back up. He wanted to vomit again; his eyes watered and saliva flooded his mouth He glanced around. His shoulders smacked into the side of the house. He felt splinters break off shingles and pierce his fingers. His nails scrabbled. He didn't know where to look.

Squash plants filled the entire back yard. *And what the fuck was that… Oh, my God, a squash the size of a submarine lumbering on tiny, clawed feet like some prehistoric alligator??* It had a strange familiarity to it, he thought, after the words 'submarine' and 'crocodilian' left his overloaded mind.

Though the head was smooth and almost featureless, Don thought he could make out where eyes would be, the mouth? *No. No. No. No. No, no, absolutely not!* The monster began to drag itself toward him using the claws on those absurdly small front feet. Don froze against the house, transfixed.

Then he over-balanced and started to fall backward through the living room window. As his hand touched glass, a huge green leaf slapped the second story window above it hard enough to create a web of cracks. One rope-thick tendril unwound from a leaf stalk and slithered toward the opening. Little pieces of broken glass bounced off the leaves, glittering as they fell.

He looked up as the green thing dragged itself closer to him. It was bizarrely beautiful, repellant but at the same time provoking protectiveness. The buzz had reached a deafening crescendo. Maggie's barking sounded faint and far away. A strange exhaustion gripped him. Don felt urged to just slide down the wall onto the grass, to forget about everything and just let the leaves wrap around his body like loving hands… he swayed on his feet.

His mail bag tripped him, and he sprawled flat on his face in front of the pulsating, oncoming giant. Pain, a knee-scraped on a rock, roused him. The tendril overhead had pushed itself through the broken window, oblivious to the weeping sap from its own skin. The scent of decay was overpowering. Another tendril unrolled itself quick as a whip across the grass, aiming for Don's face. He staggered to his feet using the rifle as a cane.

The mailman turned toward the driveway and freedom. For one brief second, he considered lifting the gun to his shoulder and firing into the oncoming mass. But no, though that thought was followed by the idea of it being an act of mercy. *Mercy??!! Where to aim?* He swiveled back and forth wildly as green that stank of dead things flowed toward his boots.

Instead, he turned and ran, rifle still in one hand, desperate to reach his vehicle. An upstairs window exploded. The sound of slithering, coming after him. Luckily, he had left the key in the ignition and the dog had not knocked it loose. He wrestled with the fucking mail bag, finally pulled it free and threw it and the firearm next to the cat carrier onto piles of mail that wasn't going to be delivered today, nope... He turned the key. Truck flooded.

"Fuck!!" he cried, tears and sweat pouring down his face, stinging his eyes. The dog's barking was earsplitting in such close confines.

"C'mon, c'mon, you son of a bitch!" he prayed, trying again and again. He knew not to touch the gas pedal, but just then the front door of the house slammed back into its frame, a green juggernaut blasting across the porch and down the steps. His foot jerked. The engine caught!

The mouth yawned open, dripping drool burning holes into anything it landed on. Grasping vines rattled toward the mail truck. One stumpy clawed arm, if you could call it that, thick around as a fence post reached through the open truck door and grabbed for his face. He ducked his head and as the claws grazed his neck, leaving a burning trail of seeping red, he saw it. Jeepers crow, a glint of silver – ring, bangle, who knew – shining from a crevasse where it had sunk into the flesh.

He shot out of the driveway in reverse and laid burnt rubber on asphalt, truck door flapping like a broken wing against the body of the vehicle. He reached out to snag it with his left hand, the right gripping the wheel so hard the skin had turned bone

white. On the highway, he slammed into drive.

Maggie braced herself, claws dug into the dashboard, barking, barking. His thigh oozed blood through his denim pants. He felt a tug on the back bumper, a sort of pulling resistance that reminded him absurdly of water skiing as a kid. He glanced in the rearview mirror and stomped the gas and the green grasper that had latched onto the bumper tore off. Thick sap bled from the wound, smoking the roadbed, melting tar. He heard the bumper clank and bounce along the road. *Tough shit, that's the government's problem!* He sped on, not knowing where they were heading, simply: Away.

As soon as he got to town, he decided to screw work and went directly home. He settled the frightened animals as best as he could and then he decided to call his nephew. He'd been puzzled ever since the dejected boy had told him that Sheryl had fired him.

"Jake, can you get over here right away?" demanded Don the second Jake picked up.

"Sure, Uncle Don. I'll just hop on my bike." But even as he finished saying the word *bike*, the connection clicked off in his ear. His heart sped up wondering why unflappable Uncle Don sounded out of breath and weird.

Don and Jake Hatch a Plan

Don scratched Maggie between her ears as he sat by the window, still in his jacket regardless of the green stains on it. He pushed the curtain aside with one finger, as if he was trying to make the image of his nephew materialize out of thin air. Soon enough Jake's familiar red head came around the curve, shoulders hunched as he gripped the handlebars and stood on the pedals, working them for all he was worth.

He dropped his bike carelessly in Don's yard and bounded up the steps two at a time. He fell into the house as Don opened the door and grabbed his arm just as he was about to knock.

Don did have one of Jake's poems stuck on his refrigerator, but it wasn't a babyish thing. He admired his nephew's ability to create such gorgeous pictures with words. Don often recalled Jake as a snot-nose toddler, baggy diaper full of... well, full, as he toddled around. Who knew that smiling little critter would grow to be a young man of such sensitivity and talent.

"What's—? Ow, my arm!" Jake rubbed his bicep

ruefully as he looked at his uncle. Normally a fairly neat guy, Don's hair was up in a mess of spikes. Green something-that-didn't-smell-very-nice smeared his jacket and one sleeve was torn. Jake could see blood and a scratch. Just then Maggie bumped her head against his thigh. Jake looked down.

"Oh hey, Mags!" His hands automatically ruffled her neck ruff. "What is she doing here?" He looked up at his uncle who was pacing back and forth in front of the window.

"Sheryl's gone missing."

"What?"

"Yeah. I went out there to deliver on my route. Had a package for her to sign. Place is neglected, door was unlocked. I went in. Total mess. Dirty dishes and clothes all over, Jeep dusty in the garage. The animals had managed to get cabinet doors open or else someone left 'em, because the bags of their food were torn open and that is how they've been eating. Toilet was up and Maggie had drunk it pretty near dry.

"Oh, my God... Gosh," Jake amended as he hugged Maggie tight. He saw Girlie hiding behind the couch, only her tail showed.

Don continued. "I walked around back, checked the barn, and then the yard. Her garden. Oh, my God, I don't know what it looked like when she let you go, but it is a jungle back there! Something came at me...." His voice trailed off. His eyes turned inward and looked glassy as he remembered being pinned against the side of the house by the enormous leaves. He glanced at Jake who was fumbling his phone out of his back pocket.

"We have to call the police, Uncle Don," he said

as he dialed 911.

Looking at this kid, white-faced, three whiskers standing out on his chin and skinny neck, even so Don could see the sensitive and gentle man he would become one day, calm in the midst of crisis. Irrelevantly Don thought, *he should be an English teacher.*

Jake was talking with the 911 operator. He tapped his phone as he hung up. The cops were on their way, coming first to Don's place.

When the state police arrived, it was Joe Dempsey and his partner Sue Willoughby, both of whom Don had gone to school with. They creaked into his apartment, crowding it with their belts and equipment and all, both of them being pretty good-sized.

Don was relieved it was these two. Joe had gone off to college and come out gay. No small thing when you grew up in a tiny conservative country town. He'd traveled some, as far as San Francisco, and eventually when his grandma took sick—she'd helped raise him and his brothers and sister, he moved back east... with a domestic partner. Phillip. Don knew his brother-in-law said gross things about gay people, but he figured that you couldn't help loving who you loved. Phillip and Joe had gotten married when the law passed. They had a nice house with a big garden and two pugs named Snickel and Fritz. Phillip was a physician's assistant and sometimes Jake's mom bumped into him if they had business at the hospital. Besides, Joe stood six-four and at two hundred twenty-five pounds, (he played football in high school), Don knew pretty much

nobody but a fool would mess with him to his face.

With no small degree of embarrassment, Don related the story of his attempt to deliver Sheryl's package and the ensuing problem. He glossed over the worst of it as he simply could not think of words to explain what had happened. Sue said that they ought to take the animals to the shelter.

"No!" Don and Jake both objected. "They know me. Us. They'll feel safe with me. Sheryl wouldn't mind. Hopefully we'll find her and she'll be glad we were able to help them out."

Sue nodded, thinking the pets were really the least of the concerns anyway.

Everything jotted down, the police said they were going to take a drive over there and see whether Don had eaten a bad burrito that gave him hallucinations (hyuck yuck) or what. They carefully made no mention of PTSD, though both of them considered it. As soon as they stumped back to their cruiser and entered some details into their dashboard laptop, Don shrugged out of his disgusting shirt.

Jake saw the cut in his arm. "You should wash that."

"Yeah, yeah, later." He jerked his arms into the sleeves of a flannel shirt that was folded in a pile of clean laundry waiting to go upstairs.

"C'mon," he nodded at his nephew as he grabbed his keys. "We're going too."

Jake was, after all, still a kid. "But they said we should stay here!"

"Okay, stay if you want. Help with the animals. Sheryl was my friend or IS. I'm going out there."

Jake shrugged into his backpack and gave Mags

one last pat. "We'll be right back, I promise."

He clipped his seatbelt as Don turned the key. Maggie stood by the living room window watching the rusty truck disappear down the road. She moaned deep in her throat. Girlie buried herself under a blanket that was hanging off the back of the couch.

Some minutes later, as the late afternoon sun was slanting through the trees and the last late crickets were tuning up, Don pulled into Sheryl's driveway. The cops were parked in front of the barn, so he drove around the circle and pulled off onto the grass so that his vehicle was not blocking theirs. As he and Jake tumbled out, they were just in time to see a uniformed back disappearing around the side of the house. Sue had gone into the house proper, gently pushing the door with her baton and with her gun holster unstrapped just in case.

"Miss Perkins? Sheryl, if you can hear me, holler." Her boots sounded loud on the wood floor. She stood in the kitchen amazed at the cupboards hanging open, the spilling bags of dog and cat chow and the mess. Dishes, trash, the stink of rotten meat.

"What the hell," she muttered under her breath. When she passed the window, she saw the top of Joe's hat bob past as he walked toward the barn. "It's bad," she said to him into her radio.

"Copy that," came his crackling reply.

When the Police Investigated

Something moved behind her, she wasn't sure if she heard a noise. She whipped out her handgun and had it in firing position, safety off. "Freeze!"

Two of the whitest white men she had ever seen looked about to wet their pants in terror as they froze alright.

"What are you all doin' here?" She was angry and could feel sweat making its way down her back into the crack of her butt. "I, we TOLD you to stay home! This is NOT your business." She was shaking her head angrily as she snapped her gun safety on, holstered the weapon.

Don looked into her dark brown eyes unwaveringly. He had nothing but respect for Sue. She had worked her ass off to make it professionally in a field that was hard for a black woman to excel in. Twenty-first century or not. She spoke into her radio with clipped tones.

"We got company, copy that."

Joe's reply was lost in static.

Jake said helpfully, "He must be in the barn. The Wi-Fi here is pretty spotty. It drives Sheryl nuts. Her

being from the city and all."

Sue glared at him "And you know this because...?"

"I worked for her nearly all summer. I helped her out in her garden, cleaned trash out of the barn, and stuff like that. Walked the dog sometimes, you know. Stuff. Summer job." He scuffed one beat up Nike over top of the other, staring at the floor between his feet. His cheeks flamed red. With inborn intuition of the sister of two younger brothers, Sue understood that Jake had a crush on this Sheryl. Poor kid. He looked to be about twelve, no older than fourteen.

"Okay, well you have to stay here. Or better still, go out and sit in the truck and wait for us. I promise we will figure this out." Just as she finished speaking, a gunshot rang out from the back yard. All three of them tore out the door and down the front porch steps.

Sue was shouting into her radio, "Joe, Joe? Come back," as she drew her own weapon. Then screaming began, followed by another gunshot.

Jake didn't think he had ever heard a human being make such a hopeless sound. Each stopped dead as if rooted to the side yard grass. They saw a dinosaur-sized green plant – *A fucking PLANT?* Sue thought – wrapping tendrils around Joe's bleeding body like some obscene spider. Don grabbed Jake so tightly that later they would find bruises across the boy's arms and chest.

"Sue! Sue DON'T get close to it! Stay back!" he wailed as she ran to help her partner. The screaming stopped. She held her pistol in one hand and bent down to touch Joe's leg with the other. He was still

120

moaning, though buried in leaves so that she couldn't see his face.

"Joe, let me help you. C'mon, Joe!" she pushed into the leaves as Jake and Don watched with horrified eyes.

"Shit! OW!" she hollered. Her eyes were stark white against her dark skin as she threw a glance over her shoulder at the two guys still frozen on the lawn.

"Stay back! Stay back!" She tried to yank her arm free. She fired her pistol into the heaving jungle. All that was left visible of Joe was one bloody boot.

Hysterically, Don thought, *Leather again. Oh. It doesn't like its meat tough.* He stifled the insane urge to giggle.

Jake gagged. He stumbled away from the garden and threw up in the driveway. Hands on his skinny knees, red hair hanging down, a string of saliva dangled from his lips.

Don turned back to Sue. He'd been counting as her weapon discharged. All her ammo was gone. Her hat had fallen from her neat dark head. She parted her hair in the middle and kept in secured in a bun at the nape of her neck. Her dad was pastor down at First Methodist. How was he going to tell him…

"Don, run!" she shouted as she pulled out her taser and zapped the leaves. One thick green tendril wrapped itself around her right leg all the way up to the thigh. Like a python it began to squeeze. Blood exploded from her thigh and poured over the green. "Get your boy outta here, Don, please!" She dropped the useless taser. "Tell Daddy I love him."

Another tendril encircled her waist and then an enormous leaf wrapped itself around her face. For a

few endless seconds it seemed she tried to keep speaking but then she must have suffocated. The whole plant seemed to pull her in and fold in upon itself.

There was silence in the late afternoon yard. Strange after all the gunshots and screams. Thick silence, no bird song, no squirrels squabbling in the trees. Don could hear Jake heaving. The tick of the cruiser's engine cooling. And then the unmistakable sound of chewing. Loud, enthusiastic crunching. He ran toward the barn and threw up, too. He grabbed Jake by an unresisting wrist and dragged him to the truck. Shoved him in and climbed in himself, aware of the surreal reality of having been through this once already. He wiped his mouth with one hand and held the steering wheel with the other. Jake fumbled with his seatbelt. Don floored it and the truck blasted out onto the highway.

After a mile or so, Don pulled onto the shoulder and turned off the truck. He rummaged in back and unearthed several bottles of warm but unopened water. He tossed one to Jake, who cracked the lid, filled his mouth and then spat the nasty residue of vomit out the window. Don did the same and then swallowed some. Water helped. They looked at each other. *Now what do we do?*

Jake started to explain to his uncle what he and Jorge had learned about this plant – if that was what it was – at the university library.

The gas gauge was almost on empty so Don put the truck in gear and they headed for a Stop 'n Shop gas station. Images of Joe and Sue and that monster plant played like a ghoulish silent movie behind

closed eyelids. After he filled up, his eyes fell on a rack of pay-as-you-go cell phones by the front register. Impulsively he grabbed one. He shoved it hastily to the cashier before she finished ringing him up, saying, "For the nephew."

The cashier who looked to be somewhere between twenty and thirty scratched her dark roots and shoved a lank lock of straw-colored hair behind her ear. One eyebrow bedecked with several rings piercing it above too much blue eye shadow raised at him in reply as if to say, *So what?*

"Thanks," muttered Don and before he had made it out the door, she'd already turned back to her smartphone, texting.

Jake looked up listlessly as Don eased back into the driver's seat groaning. "What's that?"

"I bought a burner cell. I figured we could power it up and call the cops. Call 911, fire department, whoever. Then ditch the phone and stay as far away from that place as we can."

Jake stared out the car window at the tacky, ragged display of foil garland draped over the door of the store. He nodded and said absently to his uncle, "Yeah. We can't just… leave them." An image of Sue's trooper hat bouncing across the lawn flashed in his mind and his gorge rose. He swallowed hard, willing himself not to vomit again, and turned the radio up, not caring what was on, just a thing to distract.

"Maybe the fire department guys can burn it out or something." Don shifted into gear, and they were rolling out of the parking lot. Then Jake finished telling Don about everything he and Jorge had learned about this ancient evil plant. How it only

bloomed once every seventy-five years. How it was not only neurotoxic but grew with such beauty it made a viewer feel like they must protect it at all costs. The one weakness he remembered (all too well) was how those leaves had responded to poetry being read out loud. It definitely was *not* a poetry lover.

Autumn

Seasons changed. Eventually winter came to the small mountain town. The woman writer who had lived in the house on the hill had had no children nor close friends other than the mailman and his nephew.

Jake had always wanted to ask his mom if they could invite her over for dinner someday, especially after he and she had begun discussing their poetry together. Things had deteriorated too fast for that dream to ever have come true.

She never did make it to compete in the county fair bake-off with her chocolate chip zucchini bread at the end of August either. Everyone at Larry's agreed she was a mite strange if not downright unfriendly; that way she had, for instance, of just standing on the sidewalk and staring at a person with her mouth hanging open, and nothing but your own reflection in her mirror sunglasses looking back at you. Skinnier than hell, old baggy clothing, looked like she had cancer or something.

Don thought about autumn, when she'd first moved in and word spread that they had a possible bona fide author living in their midst. Jake, who was

a few years behind Corey and Sarah in school and had aspirations of being a poet, dumb as his father found that idea, had googled her name on his laptop. Sure, enough there were a few items of interest about her and yep, she had published a few pieces, mostly in journals.

He had had a secret dream of meeting her some day and talking with her about writing. Lovingly, he had searched through his poetry journals and started to make a pile of poems to share with her. As soon as school let out, as Don remembered it, the boy would grab a PB&J for breakfast, cramming it into his mouth and mumbling, "See ya!" to his mom where she sat over the newspaper at the kitchen table with her cup of coffee. His backpack had bounced companionably against his shoulder blades. Along with his journals, he'd carried printed articles and poems he was able to find online written by or about Sheryl. He'd even showed Don a copy of a book she had written, which he'd found after a tedious internet search.

Before his uncle had helped him get the job with her, Jake had told him he'd ridden his old Raleigh down the road into sun and breeze almost every day. Casually, not daring to turn his head lest she see him looking, he'd cruised past her house, rearview mirror angled so he was able to see her front yard. Of course, if she were actually outside working—Uncle Don had told him she liked to garden—he hadn't known if he would've even been able to open his mouth to shout, "Hi" or lift an arm to wave.

The afternoon he had met her, she was carrying an armload of junk out of the barn, and he'd jammed on the brakes and flew ass-over-teakettle over the

handlebars landing in the ruts of her driveway at her feet. Sheryl had dropped the box and knelt down beside the boy.

Jake Remembers Falling in Love

"Are you okay? That was some stunt." She'd quickly decided against further embarrassing him by offering her hand to help him up. He had rolled onto his knees, a bulky backpack hanging off his right shoulder, hair in his very red face. He'd jumped to his feet, dusting his muddy hands on his jeans.

"I meant to do that," he said this with a deadpan expression.

A beat passed, then she could not help herself. Sheryl burst out laughing. Jake joined her. He stuck out a hand then looked at it, at her, and blushed beet red. He stuffed both hands in his pockets.

"Hello. Would you like to come in and wash your hands? I have Band-Aids if you need any and a pitcher of lemonade." She could see that he was fourteen, fifteen? A tall boy just starting to fill out and who had just begun to dream of shaving a microscopic patch of whiskers. His eyes were on a level with hers and a lovely green color.

"Yes, ma'am. Thank you." He hitched the pack

higher on both shoulders and rolled his bike to lean it against the barn before following her toward the porch. *Whew! Something reeked out here. Maybe an animal crawled under the floorboards to die. Yuck.* He hurried after Sheryl.

Then came the wonderful awful day that Uncle Don had called his mother to say that Sheryl was interested in hiring a guy to help with yard work and stuff. Don had suggested his nephew.

Jake continued to stare out the window as bare fields and trees flashed by. Yeah, that was something. He remembered how his heart had sped up with joy at the thought of spending time with her. He wished he could time travel back to "just before" and somehow magic away everything that had happened after.

At first, nobody but the two knew she had truly disappeared. As Don tossed and turned beneath quilted bed covers, her dog and cat stuck to his body like Velcro. He had nightmares. He went through his meager off-duty wardrobe and threw any piece of clothing remotely colored green into the burn pile behind his house.

It had to be PTSD. None of this could be real.

He stumbled out of bed, staggered to the bathroom. Opening the medicine cabinet, he took down bottles of anti-anxiety meds and others he had been able to wean off of when enough time had passed. He rattled the pills in one, looking into his bloodshot eyes in the mirror. *Nah.* He put them all back.

For a while he debated telling Jim Baker, the

local police chief. Every time he considered this, absently scratching Maggie's ears or staring into space, he always came to the conclusion that he wouldn't know how to describe what he saw in a way that wouldn't have his friend look at him with pity in his eyes. Don knew Jim was aware of his bouts with PTSD.

He couldn't be one hundred percent sure this wasn't some vestige of the war years dredged up from his subconscious. The smell of rotting meat was a trigger, memories of bodies roasting in desert sun, trapped by mortar fire behind rock barricades, unable to drag his dead buddies to safety.

One more attractive alternative would be an anonymous 911 call from a pay phone at a convenience store in another town where nobody knew him. Not that any working payphones still existed. He could just park around back and then pull his hat low and make the call. Tell the cop on the other end there was something suspicious out at the Haven place, looked vandalized. And then hang up.

He'd even gotten as far as looking for a phone booth one time, found what was probably the last surviving one in New Hampshire, had the receiver against his ear but when he heard, "What is your emergency?" he slammed it down and walked back to his truck. Because the whole northeast was madder than a hornet's nest with the news, even made national TV, of the disappearance of the two state troopers.

Trying to Cope

Jake's sleep was haunted by memories of Sue Willoughby trying to reach Joe's boot, the way she had called to Don to tell her dad she loved him. It had been all over the news, two cops disappearing out at the Haven place, possible murders. It received national attention.

Any time Jake's mom had the news on and he heard about it on TV or radio he turned it off. Don and Jake, by unspoken agreement, never discussed it. Jake tried to busy himself with schoolwork though his best friend Jorge found him withdrawn and distant, and his teachers thought he looked sick. They wondered about drugs. He spent a lot of time locked in his room, a borrowed old sweatshirt that smelled faintly of patchouli and cigarettes shoved against his face.

Don went to his job as often as he could. He took a lot of sick days though after too many sleepless nights and bad memories.

Added to those, Don knew Jake's heart had been broken as only the heart of a teen can. Recalling how, for no explicable reason, Sheryl had fired Jake at the height of summer.

After she'd fired him, Jake had moped around home until his mother, worried over with his truculence, had sent him to Don's one afternoon with a bag of tomatoes. Her tomato plants had been unusually fruitful, and she was sharing with her brother.

Don had been home, doing housework in the compulsively neat way Jake's dad always made fun of, in a mean way. Jake was no big fan of it, though he helped his mom vacuum sometimes and also knew his way around a load of laundry and how to load and run the dishwasher — *life skills*, his mom called them. But he liked Don's neat house. He always took his boots or running shoes off when he came in and lined them up next to Don's on the brightly colored rag rug next to the front door. Don was a good cook, too, and since Jake was big enough to tie a towel around himself and hold a wooden spoon, Don had taught him to make some tasty dishes.

Don had just turned off the vacuum and was coiling the cord around the handle.

Jake let himself in. He set the bag on the floor to undo his shoelaces.

"Hey, Buddy. What brings you here?" Don said as he stowed the vacuum cleaner in its place in the closet with his coats and jacket. He'd noted the pallor of Jake's fair skin and his greasy hair. He knew from talking to his sister that the summer job which seemed to have been going so well even including some poetry reading sessions between the two, had abruptly and mysteriously ended.

"Mom wanted to give you these tomatoes," he gestured with one foot toward the bag. "You make

better sauce than she does." Jake straightened up.

Don looked at him. "You want to tell me about it?"

"What?" Jake slouched into his favorite easy chair.

"What?! Your summer job that's what! What happened? I thought you and Sheryl got along like two ticks on a dog's tail. Reading your poems to her even?"

Jake slid even lower into the chair cushions, if that was possible. His chin disappeared into the neck of his stretched-out tee shirt.

Don went into the kitchen to start a pot of coffee. The good homey smell of grounds filled the room. "You want a piece of pie? I made apple."

One shoulder twitched.

"I'll take that as a 'yes' and here is some milk to go with it." He set two plates and silverware on the placemats on his table. Set the glass of milk at Jake's accustomed place. "Now spill, dude."

Jake Spills

Jake heaved himself out of the cushions like an old man. He sighed as he shuffled over to his chair. Sat down harder than he meant to on the wood and mumbled "Ouch."

He picked up his fork as Don set a slice of warmed pie onto his plate. He held the fork and stared as if he'd never seen one before.

"Your mom would kill me, but what the fuck, dude?"

Much to his own horror, Jake started to cry. Once he felt the tears' hot trails down his cheeks, he couldn't stop. He laid his head on his arms.

"Hey, buddy, little buddy," Don murmured as he dragged his own chair next to Jake and circled the skinny shoulders with one arm. He tried to pry Jake's face out of his placemat with one hand. "Let me get some Kleenex." He stood and walked to the bathroom.

When he returned Jake had scrubbed his face with his sleeves and was at least sitting upright. Looked like the pie was going to be a bust though.

Don pushed the Kleenex box toward the boy. He

felt a momentary surge of anger at Sheryl for breaking this kid's heart. At least that was what he suspected had happened. Jake was a good worker and dependable. He was pretty sure whatever it was had not been because of something Jake had done. He remembered a strange aloofness, a downright unfriendliness coming from Sheryl over time. Days she refused to answer the door when he knocked just to say 'hey'. Or if she did come out at least to pretend to be neighborly with a lemonade for Don, he recalled she'd gotten awfully thin and her skin had taken on an unhealthy pallor. He had wondered if she was sick but hadn't felt comfortable asking.

Jake stuttered to begin. "Everything was great. She liked me, I could tell. I did every job she asked me to. She liked it that I was good with her dog and cat, too. I love Maggie."

"Me, too," agreed Don.

"Anyway, we used to sit after working and drink lemonade or sometimes we'd have a brush fire and we'd toast marshmallows for a snack. She talked to me like I was, you know, a person, not just a kid. We talked about poetry and books and what her life in the big city was like." His eyes grew shiny at the memories.

Don thought, *Poor boy. Puppy love hurts.*

"You know how awful my dad is about my poetry writing. One time he even took my notebook of poems and threw it in the recycling bin on trash day."

Don nodded. What an ass Larry could be.

"Well, I brought her some poems and one day even though I was scared to, I asked her if I could read

her one or if not, would she read one of mine. She said yes!" For a moment it was as if the sun had broken through, shining on the boy's face, wonderment that this hero he admired would actually be interested in his words.

"She liked what I wrote Uncle Don! She really did. But like a grownup, you get it? She didn't just tell me *good job* like people do to a toddler who just pooped in the toilet."

Don grinned at that.

Jake smiled, "For real she would explain what she liked and why and then she might suggest other ways to say stuff or other kinds of words to use. She never made me feel embarrassed or ashamed. I didn't always have to agree with her either. She told me that. She said when someone gives you a critique, which is not criticism, it's something different, it doesn't mean they're right or wrong it is just their opinion. You own your own words and so you get to pick and choose from this critique on what you think might work for you." Here he looked up from the table and his face was suffused with pride. "She was... she is... amazing."

Don rubbed his head and glanced at the coffee pot. "Yep. She is that buddy."

"But then one day she started to sorta get sick, I guess. She didn't look too good, and she didn't want to sit and have poetry and marshmallows anymore. At first, she decided we could only read inside. She said she didn't want me to go into the back garden anymore either. Started just leaving me a list of chores stuck to the front door with a tack. Then one day there wasn't a list. I knocked and knocked. I could hear

Maggie barking in there. Finally, I rode away. I came back the next day on time like I was supposed to, and when I knocked, she opened the door so hard I almost fell. She shouted mean stuff to the dog and when she looked at me, she looked like a stranger. Her clothes were baggy and kinda dirty and her hair, and she was so skinny. I was scared. Of her, for her. Something was wrong. Then she just said, *I don't need your help anymore,* shoved a wad of cash into my hand and slammed the door in my face."

Don was stricken at the pain his nephew had suffered.

"I just stood there like a doofus with that cash in my hand. My heart was pounding in my chest so hard. That terrible smell like a swamp or a bad septic stink was everywhere. Finally, I dropped the cash between the storm door and the other door which was locked, and got on my bike and left.

Don's mind had been blown. It was strange information, but it felt right. The two had talked a while longer, hugged, and then Don had sent Jake on his way.

Halloween came and went, followed by Thanksgiving. The unease of Sheryl's disappearance lingered. His sister invited Don to their house for turkey. He hated to go be around her husband but went for her sake and the boy. At least there was a football game on pretty much nonstop.

Christmas Season Approaches

Then the holiday rush began for Don at work. Jake had end of semester projects and papers at school. Mrs. Gomez had encouraged him to submit some poems for publication. She showed him how to find likely markets. Right before Christmas, he received an email from a mid-level literary journal. His poem, accepted!

His mom decided then and there that in the next few years she was going to make sure her son went to college for English. Good teachers are always in demand and Larry could just stuff it.

Don was offered a new position with a better pay grade at a post office in a neighboring town maybe forty-five minutes away. His old and new bosses both apologized for the inconvenience of springing this on him at holiday time which was the absolute worst part of the US Mail Service's year. He didn't care. He jumped at the chance to leave. To pack up the dog, cat, and his belongings and to move on, maybe outrun the memories.

Too strange for them to discuss even though both guys' dreams were haunted and their waking

thoughts filled with anxiety, wondering where Sheryl had gone and what had happened to her that day in her yard, the cops and all. Nothing like that could possibly be real, right?

As Don finished loading boxes and carryalls into his truck, Jake rode his bike through the slush up the driveway.

The Goodbye Lunch

"Hey, Uncle Don," he called out.

Winter was late this year, unusually warm. Some trees still held a few handfuls of leaves and the ground was mostly green and brown with only an occasional puddle of snow splotch. Some plants that would've been killed by frost were still hanging on.

Don turned around as he slammed the truck gate shut. Maggie heaved herself to her feet and climbed off the porch to wag over to Jake. The boy laughed, then suddenly bent over as she jammed her nose into the crotch of his jeans.

"Maggie! That isn't polite," Don laughed, too. Dogs were honest.

Through all the sleepless nights and bad dreams, the one person he had contemplated talking about that day with was this young man in front of him. After all, he had been there.

Seized by a sudden impulse, Don asked, "You want to go into town for a cuppa joe, grab lunch, donut, something?"

Jake looked up at his uncle from where he squatted hugging Maggie. She smelled a little bit like

old cheese. His mom told him once dogs that spent lots of time in the water did stink that way.

"You need a bath, Maggie," he told her digging one linty dog bone out of his back pocket. He offered it to her. Maggie took it gently between her worn down old teeth and ambled back to the porch.

"Sure. I wish you weren't moving." The boy looked momentarily sad, scuffing his boots and kicking a tire lightly.

Don said nothing just climbed into the truck and waited for Jake to do the same, snapping his seatbelt before turning the key. Jake fiddled with the radio. They drove west toward Bennington. There was a nice diner simply called *Mom's* he was especially fond of. They served a mean pot roast with gravy. This wet day was a hot lunch kind of day if ever there was one.

The waitress looked up as they walked in, stomped off their boots on the big mat. "Hey Don-boy. You know the drill."

The place wasn't very busy, it being so close to Christmas, so they had their pick of tables. Don chose one as far from the counter as possible, in an alcove with a window and deep booth seats. "This okay?"

He didn't expect Jake to say it wasn't. They slid in and their server came over to set napkin-wrapped silverware and glasses of ice water in front of them.

"What'll it be, boys?" she asked, shoving her hair behind her ear with one hand, pad in the other. She couldn't wait to get it cut. Those bangs were driving her nuts.

Don had had the taste for the hot roast beef ever since he thought of it, and Jake ordered a fried fish

dinner. At forty-six, Don remembered very well the hunger of a teenaged boy. "Get a bunch of sides, too, Jakey." So, Jake added on applesauce, coleslaw, double fries, and a plate of onion rings.

He grinned at his uncle, "I'll share the rings with you."

"S'okay, dude. Onions and me don't get along like we used to."

As soon as the waitress disappeared into the kitchen through the swinging silver door, Don slumped in his seat. He sipped his water and stared out the window.

Most boys are pretty self-absorbed but Jake was a poet. Though he took a lot of crap for this from his dad and brother, his mom had taken him aside one day and told him that poets have an extra tool to deal with the hardship and pain that is life.

"You all can make word pictures and color them with feelings that the rest of us can relate to even if we couldn't do it to save our own lives."

Jake could not fail to notice his uncle seemed down rather than excited about moving to a new place.

The Making of White Magic: A Weapon

The waitress returned placing plate after plate of Jake's sides in front of him.

"Uncle Don," Jake began, mouth full of fries.

"Ye-es." Don didn't like the look in Jake's eyes.

"We gotta go back out there," he swallowed.

Don lost his appetite.

"Hell, you say, sonny-boy. Why on earth would we do that?"

"Well, the cops don't bother much anymore, right? Didn't you tell me you had a funny feeling that there was something off about that place from a long time ago? Didn't you tell me after that, you know, day, that you had searched county records as far back as they went to see if you could find any Haven folks?"

Reluctantly Don admitted he had. He'd never found a record of any family named Haven living there.

"How can you just leave it? What happened to her? Jorge and I've been looking around on the

143

Internet. I think I know a way we might be able to kill it or send it back where it came from."

"You told Jorge?"

"Yeah sorta, a little bit. Don't worry, he's cool. He's really a techie geek, so I asked his help."

"Seriously, dude?"

"Yes, seriously. We just have to get a bunch of poetry books. You got any?"

"Poetry books? Poetry books! Dog, you crazy!"

"No, I'm not. I don't know that this would work but it's worth a try. I have a feeling."

Don took a bite of his lunch. He chewed, casting his mind back to his house before he'd packed everything up and to the bookshelves. Being a neat fellow, he knew exactly where the boxes with books were stacked. Yes, he had a few poetry collections or anthologies, whatever the hell you call 'em, left from high school. And when Jake had begun to show promise as a poet, he'd gone to the used book section on Amazon and found a few more. Poets like Marge Piercy, WD Snodgrass, Maya Angelou, a book of poems written by soldiers in Viet Nam.

They finished their lunch and wished the waitress happy holidays. Back at Don's box-stacked house, they rooted through until he found the boxes marked *Books* in sharpie. They ripped open the packing tape. Soon a small pile of poetry lay strewn around their feet on the floor.

Jake stuffed the slim volumes into his backpack, resisting the urge to stop and peruse the contents. Poetry had a seductive hold on this boy's heart, and he knew once you began to read, it was as if a magic spell took hold of you and held you captive.

As he buckled his pack shut, he thought, *At least I hope so... strong enough magic to captivate more than just me.*

He patted his own back pocket where a fat wad of folded poems he'd written resided more or less permanently. He felt naked if he didn't have his poems in his pocket. He loved April which was national poetry month and that particular day toward the end of the month, "Poem in Your Pocket Day."

No doubt about it. Poetry had power. Even the president of the United States had a poet read at their inauguration. The question remained: just how much power?

The man and the boy did not speak as they rode down the familiar country byways to reach the Haven house. Jake's signed copy of her book *Transplanted* was also tucked into his pack. Radio off, no sound but the wind rushing past and the slightly rough sound of the engine.

Needs a tune up, thought Don absently.

Too soon they saw the roof of the barn up ahead and then the end of her driveway with the mailbox that said "Perkins" in slightly crooked letters. A gust of sadness swept over Don.

Jake felt it. He had loved her, too. Not that someone like her would've ever, you know, liked a guy his age that way, but she had been special in his eyes. And maybe she and Uncle Don could've been a couple. Now they'd never know.

Don stopped and Jake got out to move the sawhorses and orange hazard cones out of the way at the end of the driveway so they could pull in. He left them in the grass. If his plan worked, they'd be

leaving again real soon. He whipped out his iPhone and texted Jorge a quick emoji of crossed fingers. His phone dinged right back, a fist bump emoji and a thumbs up. Jake slid it back into his pocket.

Jorge was their insurance. He had promised to call for help if he didn't hear from Jake by bedtime. Even now, Jorge sat in his room, listening to his sister giggling with her friend downstairs, breathing in the scent of simmering enchiladas and Pico de Gallo, which normally would've left his mouth watering, but because of the part he played in his friend's quest, made him feel a bit nauseated instead.

He and Jake had briefly considered building some sort of harness out of duct tape so Jake could wear his iPhone facing out with the video on so that Jorge would see what they saw. In the end it just seemed simpler to wait it out blind.

"Besides, 'Mano," Jake said the last time they spoke, "What we saw… you don't want that in your dreams, man."

The house stood mute, paint peeling, porch sagging. Ruts in the driveway collected water where the tow truck had hauled the cops' cruiser out of there. Bits of yellow police tape fluttered in the wind, torn and beginning to fade. A shiny new lock was screwed to the front door. The faint odor of rotting meat floated in the air.

Once they got out, Don pocketed his keys, and the boy took the books from his backpack. He divided them between his uncle and himself. They bumped fists and then Don grabbed him in a tight hug like he used to when Jake was a tiny boy.

"Let's do it."

Shoulder to shoulder they marched to the back yard.

It was waiting for them.

Powerful Magic: Poetry

While the rest of the natural world was winding down to winter sleep, the green monstrosity was as vibrant as ever. Unwillingly, Don remembered the glint of a sliver bangle embedded deep in that awful flesh. Sheryl loved silver. She always said, when he complimented her jewelry, that she was a cheap date for herself because gold held little appeal, but silver, now *that* was the metal made of moonlight... and the moon was her birth planet.

Damn, he thought as he angrily brushed a tear off his cheek.

They spread out and crept as close as they could to the quivering giant. It sensed them. Leaves rustled, seeming to whisper, *Juicy, how juuuuicccy*. Jake shook his head aware that it was important not to listen. That buzzing sound hurt his ears. He pulled out a book just as a fat tendril disengaged itself from the stalk around which it had been wrapped and rolled toward his sneaker feet.

He shouted, "Sheryl! This is for you. We love you! Be free!" And he began to read aloud. To his left Don did the same, holding the book, because he was

farsighted, away from him like a battle shield.

The leaves hissed and snapped. Tendrils uncoiled and then pulled back in on themselves. The stench intensified so badly the two almost couldn't breathe. Jake was prepared.

"Get your mask!" he shouted to Don as he yanked a white face mask, the kind you use for painting and sanding, over his mouth and nose. In just that infinitesimal pause, vines whipped back out to grip his foot. It hurt, oh, gosh it hurt so bad, but the young man ignored it and shouted the next poem into the beast.

Across Town; Maggie and Girlie

At the exact time that Jake and Don began to recite poetry, at home, Maggie, who had been resisting a doze on Don's couch shook herself to alertness. Girlie crouched in the windowsill next to Maggie's head. The two looked at each other. They had been together since babyhood. Without any conversation of the kind humans might engage in, they had always understood that God had sent them to accompany this woman and to protect her all her days upon the Earth. All dogs and cats understand this.

The best times were when she said the words "bye-bye" and "car." Girlie didn't like car rides of course, but Maggie felt life was perfect when she and her pack leader went out in the world together, whether walking through the many city parks or in the car. Except to the vet. No sane animal ever wants to see the vet no matter how many treats they give there. It's all a lie to disguise the needles.

When they lived in the place called "city" and

Sheryl left every morning to go to a place she called "work" or "job" she had always paused with her keys in hand, one hand on the doorknob, then turn back to touch both Girlie and Maggie and she'd always promised, "I will be right back."

The thing humans believe that Maggie knew was incorrect, was that once a human left a dog or cat and went away somewhere, the animal forgot the existence of the human. They said that was the reason a dog was so happy to see them when they returned home. Or that a cat was so happy she sulked in the corner for a suitable amount of time to teach the human a lesson before considering letting herself be petted and fussed over as was her due.

Maggie and Girlie felt the soul connection to Sheryl no matter whether they were physically together, no matter if they were asleep and walking in dreams — a dog could follow a human into dream territory — and no matter how far away she went to "job." Maggie felt the exact moments when Sheryl put on her coat and grabbed her purse to walk to the parking lot where she kept her car at "job." Maggie would get up and begin pacing, wagging her tail near the door of their apartment and whining softly at least twenty minutes before Sheryl's key touched the lock. Girlie's pupils would enlarge and darken and sometimes she set aside her dignity and would pounce on Maggie's tail.

Maggie had felt a lot of hope when Sheryl told them she had left "job" for good. Mags was sure that meant they would all be together all day and that was best when you were charged by Spirit with the guardianship of another life. Then Sheryl told them

she had found them a house and that they would be moving from the noisy, smelly city to "country" whatever that was, and that the new house had a "yard." Yard, Sheryl had explained to her elderly dog, was like "park" only better because it was yours and no other dogs peed there, and you could lie in the sun without worrying about strangers talking to you or cars coming by.

They both had had hope when they considered this new place. Sheryl's energy seemed lighter and freer as she packed boxes. Neither animal liked that part. It was anxiety-producing having all the familiar-smelling objects put in anonymous brown boxes that stank of dead trees.

Day by day as Sheryl had boxed up the apartment, there were fewer and fewer places to lie down in comfort. The last day, all they had was the bed the three shared and their food bowls, Sheryl's coffee maker, and one mug.

Then they traveled a very long time in "car" (especially annoying for Girlie, locked in her carry crate) until they arrived at "house."

At first, they were enchanted. It was so quiet that they could listen to wind and birds and hear mice creeping deep in the earth beneath the grass. Sheryl had been right. As she walked around the yard, no scent of other dogs was there. Coyote some days and sometimes a fox message, and fascinating fragrances of dead rodents and squirrel and rabbit poop and other such delicacies. On a good day, Maggie was able to fit in a wallow rolling in a dead chipmunk before Sheryl discovered her. After, it was always "bath." But for as long as the perfume of dead chipmunk was

rubbed into her neck fur, she felt sublime.

She never felt quite comfortable near the other building, the one Sheryl called "barn." Something evil had been there and traces of that lingered. Maggie's heart had sunk when Sheryl became determined to clear out all the old junk in there. And the day her woman found that strange packet of seeds was, for Maggie and Girlie, the true beginning of the end.

Sheryl lacked a certain awareness that all animals have because she was only human. The two of them tried their best – whether by misbehaving or playing – to distract her from going out there. One time Maggie tried to drag the seed packet out of Sheryl's jeans to bury it in the woods. Nothing worked. Sheryl was vulnerable and consequently they were helpless. The evil that emanated from those seeds snuck into Maggie's dreams. *You are a powerless old dog now. Toothless. You can do nothing,* it whispered through her dreaming mind.

Today the pair waited for the man and the boy. The moment Jake spoke the first words of poetry in Sheryl's back yard, Maggie's head came up and she barked.

Jake finished the first book, threw it to the ground, and began the second. Don was reading as if his life depended on it, which, in fact, it did. All that kept them safe from the thing that had taken the woman they had both loved, who had been absorbed by an ancient evil, a revenant in the earth itself and older than the boulders surrounding the property, were the words of poets. Some little or unknown, it didn't matter. Jake screamed Emily Dickinson, Audre

Lourde, and Maya Angelou into the mass of oncoming leaves that threatened to drop down over his head and suffocate him. He could hear the piano poem by Bruce Smith as Uncle Don recited it at the top of his lungs. The grip on his foot eased up. He felt the tendril quiver as if it was weakening. Pierre Reverdie's surrealistic poetry added more strength to their power.

They had agreed ahead that if they ran out of books to just start over and read them all again and again, as long as it took. If it didn't work, well, they would be able to tell and had decided in that awful event to run like hell.

It did work. The poets' words read with passion and fear evolved into joy and sorrow. The giant leaves began to crinkle at their edges, to fold in on themselves and wither. Tears and sweat poured down Jake's face as he read from the much-folded packet of his own poems, some inspired by and shared with Sheryl, but even though half-blinded, he knew those words by heart, and he saw the deepening wrinkles in the trunks of the monster.

The thing began to look like just a plant. It shrank and shivered as words wove a visible sparkling net of magic in the air around them. Jake read some of Sheryl's work and some of his own love poems to her. The two read until their voices grew hoarse and throats sore and then they whispered those words of power. The sparkling net strengthened and took on the appearance of stainless steel. Over and around them, this shield grew to an impenetrable, blinding bright cloud. No one outside could've seen them inside it. Electricity zipped all

over the surface, sparking and snapping but they were not burned. Winds thrashed the trees. Thunder cracked.

Suddenly, the earth trembled as if with an earthquake and right before their exhausted eyes, a huge crack yawned open. The vestiges of an abnormally large zucchini — though they both knew it had never been a squash plant, not really — vanished into the depths of a sink hole.

There was one last deafening thunder clap that left their ears feeling stuffed with cotton. Lightning flashed, blinding their vision for a moment. A drenching downpour that felt strangely warm for December soothed their aching bodies. Neither moved, grateful for the warmth and welcome wetness, tongues stuck out to catch droplets for parched throats. Then it passed as such weather phenomena do.

When they could see the yard and each other again, the sparkling net overhead was gone. Had it been a cloud? A rainbow? Neither knew. But it *had* been real.

Jake was carefully stuffing the books, which somehow were not wet from the cloudburst, one at a time (so no pages or covers bent) into his jacket to protect them.

Nothing remained of the garden but a bare patch of earth, slightly mounded, surrounded by a box of cedar planks waiting for and dreaming of spring. Something half-buried in the soil gleamed. Hesitantly Jake stepped over the planks and bent down. His fingers dug around it and loosened the object. He held it out to Don with one hand, eyes round in

wonderment. As he brushed off crumbs of dirt with the other, they both gazed at the tarnished silver bangle bracelet.

At the exact moment Jake laid the tarnished silver bracelet that Sheryl had worn all the days of her life (even when Maggie had been a teething puppy) in his uncle's warm palm, across town Maggie lifted her nose to the sky and howled. Girlie threw herself on her back on the rug and rolled like a kitten. In the silence that followed, both animals felt for the first time in many months the touch of beloved hands and heard whispered words, "I'll be right back."

Don and Jake threw their arms around each other and sobbed like babies for a minute. They let go and looked at each other. Jake started to laugh.

"My dad," he chuckled, "my dad thinks poets are so gay. He would think *we* are so gay!"

Even though his brother-in-law's ignorance and narrow worldview was not, in fact, funny, this afternoon Don laughed so hard the tears streamed down his cheeks again.

Hitching and hiccupping they turned away from the garden. "Let's go home. Time to feed Maggie and Girlie and take the dog for her walk."

As they got into the truck for the last time. Don said, "Better text Jorge."

Afterword

The old house on the hill peeled its paint under snow and sun, rain and drought. Leaves carpeted the yard, reds, golds, and rusty oranges. All were eventually buried beneath winter's fierce white serenity. Killing frost had taken the garden while the last leaves still clung to the sugar maples.

Jake and Don had decided to take the bracelet to a jeweler and to have it melted down to be fashioned into a pendant for Maggie to wear with her dog tags. It looked like a woman's smiling face.

Don did move away, but Jake was able to catch a bus ride on weekends to go visit. Sometimes Jorge came with him.

Jake asked Jorge to teach him some Spanish expressions. The boys were especially fond of swears. It was their habit to wear their hoodies up with sunglasses, pants down below their hips baggily hanging on by a prayer and optimism, and to slouch in the back of the bus chattering in Spanish conversation. It never occurred to them some adult on the bus might also be a Spanish speaker. They laughed a lot.

Maggie and Girlie always were restless at least a half hour before Jake's key turned in the lock. One night he summoned the courage to pull that precious surviving manuscript of Sheryl's out from between his mattress and box spring. Shrugging into the sweatshirt that smelled like her, he opened the folder. The words jumped out at him "To my good friend, Jake. Thank you for coming into my life and bringing me back to poetry. You are my Muse. With love."

He would ask Mrs. Gomez to help him find a way to get it published.

Winter flattened everything. The following spring, weeds poked tiny spears above the crusted earth bit by bit. Nothing remained of a woman's once riotously-fecund garden but a slightly heaved up cedar frame, four squares that combined made a larger plot. A person seeing it might be curious, "I wonder what they grew here?"

That far-off day when the mailman had made his final delivery to the Haven house, the squash plant had reached the barn door and shoved its mindless way in, taking up all the space where farm equipment used to live. One smallish female blossom with fingerling base had opened, and pollen from a male flower just outside blew in on a chill wind. After fertilization, she grew fat and lived just long enough to make seeds, until she fell off her stalk onto a dusty shelf on the back wall. Just under the shelf lay a shabby old cardboard box. Through the winter her flesh froze, rotted and fell away, leaving behind five shiny seeds that made small *pop* sounds as they dropped one by one into the container. A pair of almost-new garden gloves and a still-shiny trowel lay

on the table next to the shelf. Dust sifted down from the barn rafters to cover everything with a thin film, disturbed perhaps, by bats or mice or roosting pigeons.

Just a little bit too far from where Jake and Don had stood shouting, this piece of the monster was not much affected by the poetry. There had been a strong breeze that afternoon. Wind direction changed with certain gusts, and while a stanza of a poem might've been audible in the shadows of the barn for a moment, the seeds had clattered, clumped in their box as the contents shifted. One shiny white skin cracked when a line from Marge Piercy floated in the door. The wind changed direction as winds often do. Winnie the Pooh knew what he was talking about describing it as blustery. Then it changed yet again and another couple lines from Henri Cole echoed in the empty barn. Two more seeds' skins shriveled. The one that cracked developed black spots. The wind died down, and birdsong took its place. The reciters or as they thought of themselves, the guardians, had finished their final poem by Patricia Smith and had driven away in Don's old truck.

The following year, on a Tuesday morning in March, when spring promised everything, as she always does, a young Boston couple telephoned a small-town New Hampshire realtor. They were hoping to find an old farmhouse, ideally with outbuildings—they were both artists and wanted a barn to renovate for studio space. The realtor checked listings on her iPad.

"Sure," she said into the phone as she looked at a photo onscreen of the house on the hill. "I know just

the place, the old Haven homestead."

The young woman replied, "Great! Oh, and also, we love to garden."

Author's Note

This story was ten years in the making. Interrupted by multiple moves, break-ups, and deaths. Nonetheless, at long last, here it is.

I would like to thank my cousin Jennifer Hubbard Brooks, who read the very first versions of it and was totally encouraging. My friend, author Judy McGinn, who was the only other beta reader and was equally enthusiastic. I am so sorry they are no longer here to see the finished project.

Others to whom I owe a lot are my friend and colleague, Candice Louisa Daquin. Also, workshop leaders Ethel Rohan, Jane Smiley, and Michael Czarnecki - from whom I studied multiple types of prose writing through the years - and fellow students in those classes.

Thanks *Coast to Coast Poets* and Len Germinara.

I can't leave out the Canastota Writers Group, those wonderful folks who (back when I lived in Erieville, New York) listened to some of the earliest scenes when I was first finding my voice. Or Elizabeth R. Patton, Laura Williams French, and all the woman-owned small presses and journals who take risks on my work. Katherine Grace McDaniel, Sharon Knutson.

Thank you, Tara.

Thanks Tom O'Connor.

Thank you to my cats Nestlé, Katie, and Gabby, in particular, for keeping my heart beating. Thank you to my old black Lab, Annie, (and all the others) who guarded my life with her own.

Last but not least, thanks to you, Constant Reader. Those who come out in blizzards and downpours to listen, buy books, and reach out with kind words after reading. Who do interviews, podcasts, and write reviews.

I do have a big garden and had read Marge Piercy's poem "The Zucchini People" years ago. The first summer in this house, 2017, I looked out the upstairs window and saw my own squash plants, big as helicopters, on the lawn, I thought of that poem and then my story continued on its own journey.

Any scientific information that the boys discover about the squash is totally my own invention.

If you or someone you know needs help, call the National Mental Health hotline 866-903-3787.

About the Author

Rachael Ikins is an activist, 2016/18 Pushcart, 2013/18 CNY Book Award nominee, 2018 Independent Book Award winner, & 2019 Vinnie Ream & 2019/2021 Faulkner finalist. A 2021 Best of the Net nominee, 2023 Editors Choice Award from Studio B. October 2023 2nd prize and an HM from Northwind Writing Competition sponsored by Raw Earth Ink, Alaska. 2024 HM Northwind Writing Award and three Pushcart nominations.

A graduate of Syracuse University with a degree in Child and Family Studies, Ikins worked as a sign language interpreter for deaf students ages K-12 and also as a veterinary technician before devoting herself full time to writing.

Fellowships: Colgate Writers Conferences for poetry (3) and young adult literature.

She founded and moderated the feature/open mic event bimonthly Monday Night Poetry at a sushi blues 2008-2011.

Honorarium from Finishing Line Press for a week-long workshop in Lismore Castle, Lismore, Ireland 2014. While there she worked with Patricia Smith, Jane Smiley, Ethel Rohan and others. June 2014 she juried into Marge Piercy's Poetry Intensive workshop, Cape Cod. Post Covid she studied via zoom with Craig Czury for several years.

Ikins is a Fingerlakes-born author and illustrator of multiple books in multiple genres. Her work appears in journals such as the *Muddy River Poetry Review, Owl Light, Literary Turning Points,The Mason Street Review, Broadkill Review,* Fly on the Wall Press UK, *Synkroniciti, the Red Wheelbarrow, S/tick, Dragon Poet Review, Indigo Blue online UK, Cider Press Review, Masticadores Canada. Panoply Review, Syracuse Poster Project, The Healing Muse, The Pen Woman Magazine, Avocet,* Moonstone Press, anthologies from IndieBlue Press, *The Brave* (Clare Songbirds Publishing House), *Spontaneity Review,* Ireland, and many others. Her poetry has been translated into Gaelic.

Her visual art and photography has won prizes and hung in galleries from CNY to Washington DC and appeared on local television stations and on many journal covers. She is a member of NLAPW and The Sage Creators Collective. She works as associate contributing editor at Clare Songbirds Publishing House and has signed with October City Press, Chicago.

Ikins also spends significant time mentoring emerging poets and helping them achieve published works. She can be reached at rachaelikins@gmail.com if you wish to hire her services.

She has appeared on the New York Parrot Literary Review YouTube, podcasts, and in other interviews.

Find her
@rzikins.author.artist (Instagram)
At: *Rachael Ikins Books and Poetry* and *Ask the Girl Arts* (Facebook)

www.ingramcontent.com/pod-product-compliance
Lightning Source LLC
Chambersburg PA
CBHW051826170626
46807CB00003B/1053